Magic and Mayhem in Misty Vale
A Misty Vale Cozy Mystery
Book 2
Sarah Lewin © 2025

---

1. http://www.sarahlewin.com

This book is dedicated to:
Authors who inspire a sense of mischief, magic, and mystery
My teachers, parents, and author friends
My four beautiful grown-up children and my amazingly patient husband
And my friends who I have met along my journey
I am who I am today, because of you

Chapter One

I stared at the dark grey metal trinket box in my hands. The artefact hand forged several generations ago by one of my ancestors was over two hundred years old. Wrapped around the outside lay another layer of metal, an intricate web of rose petals, leaves and stems, peppered with thorns. A jewellery box created in an age when magic was commonplace. The intricate design included crystals that represented the five elements. The ruby for fire, the lapis lazuli for water, an emerald for earth, and an opal for air. The amethyst, for the spirit, lay boldly in the middle of the rose petals.

My grandmother Hazel, who I'd only recently become acquainted with, passed it to me at dinner the night before. "This box was made for you," she told me, pointing to the name Clara Thorne embroidered into the lining of the box over a hundred years before my birth. Having spent most of my thirty plus year believing my name to be Jane Fairweather, I only became aware of my true identity and destiny when I arrived in Misty Vale. Neither of my parents talked of the past, leading me to believe there were no other family members in our tree. Worse still, they didn't teach me about the elemental magic that ran deep in our veins. I spent most of my life thinking there was something terribly wrong with me.

I'd finally fallen asleep with the trinket box sitting on my lap, until my cat, a lightly gingery coloured feline named Cinnamon nudged it away to take her spot on the bed.

Now, hours later, she watched me as I swung my legs over the side of the bed, running my hand over the intricately fashioned box. My brown and white terrier pup, Sprinkles stared at me, his tail waving eagerly.

"Grandma is certain I'll work out how to open this," I told my furry family as I pointed to a small hidden compartment on the inside of the box. The purple fabric lining lifted back to reveal a little drawer, without any discernible way to open it. The bottom of the box didn't provide any clues. Sprinkles and Cinnamon sat in front of me, expectantly. "I know it's breakfast time. I'll be there in a minute." I moved my hands over the box. "My powers are stronger, and with Hazel teaching me, I haven't caused any freak storms for a couple of weeks." I hadn't short circuited any electrical appliances either, but as I was on my way to the kitchen to turn on the kettle, I didn't want to jinx myself. Sprinkles yawned, Cinnamon rubbed her back against my legs. "Okay, okay, I'll feed you guys." My crazy pup and more refined cat followed me to the kitchen in my cute little cottage. Bert the budgie tweeted his greeting.

After clicking the button on the kettle, I ducked into the bathroom to splash water on my face. My green-brown eyes stared back at me from the mirror. My brown hair, with the faint strand of grey starting to come through, was still in yesterday's ponytail. Did I look nearly forty? I poked the skin on my face with my fingers. My normally pale skin was a little more tanned and lightly freckled since I returned to Australia. Even more so, in Misty Vale where I made a point to walk everywhere.

Once the kettle boiled, I sat at my kitchen table with a peppermint tea as my menagerie licked, chomped, and pecked their way through their breakfast. My eyes returned to the rectangular box. "Grandma didn't say much about it, except that this has been handed down through three, now four generations," I told my animals as they finished munching their morning meal. I couldn't see a keyhole or any sort of opening to leverage the secret compartment. The box wasn't particularly heavy. It fitted neatly in the palm of my hand. Whatever hid inside wasn't large.

The grey metal of my crystal ring glinted, catching my eye. Did the same ancestor who created the box make my ring? This piece of jewellery had made its way from Misty Vale to the large country town where I grew up, travelling with me as I lived and worked overseas. It remained hidden in a box of childhood memories, until a week before Christmas when I needed it, to prove my identity. "It's funny how things turn out." Cinnamon glanced at me as I mused aloud. "Either this travelled with me for years as I searched for a place to call home, or it showed up here, because I found one."

Five small stones sat encased in the dull metal of my antique grey metal ring. A small red stone sat alongside a small green one, followed by a blue stone, an amber coloured stone, with a purple stone completing the circle. On the day I found it, I slid it onto the ring finger on my right hand, and there it remained.

I yawned. My sleep patterns hadn't improved since moving to Misty Vale. A life of running away from my fears, meant my nights were often full of being chased, ridiculed, ostracised and hunted. Anxiety played a part too, though I rarely admitted it out loud. I never made enough friends to care about how I appeared to others. "I told myself I wasn't running, or scared of being ridiculed and bullied for being different," I told Bert. "A long time ago, my fiancé called off the wedding. He called me crazy. Neither of us understood why storms and electricity went hay wire when I was upset. I decided to find a career I could throw myself into." Bert chirped conversationally as I continued to talk aloud, a habit I developed years ago. Talking to myself, before I found my menagerie, helped me ease my anxious thoughts. "As a police officer in the UK it was easy to get moved around, with secondments into parts of Europe too. After one too many incidents where my untamed magic caused chaos, I opted for a more solitary life as a private investigator. Until I found home here, and my family."

There was time before my morning meeting, for at least one coffee. I couldn't afford to sound half asleep or distracted when I met the Midsummer Moonlight Masquerade committee. When I first arrived in Misty Vale, I became acquainted with members of the local book club. "That wasn't the best choice, considering Florence ended up going to gaol, and Marigold, Constance and Gwennie have since cancelled the book club. My grandmother and I had been instrumental in uncovering Florence's criminal behaviour. It's no wonder I'm no longer welcome." I shrugged my shoulders and sighed. "The book club members were all at least fifteen years older than me. Grandma suggested I get to know some people my own age." I told Bert. Cinnamon and Sprinkles had disappeared through the animal flap for their morning sunshine quota. My stomach felt like hundreds of butterflies were stampeding. It'd be easy to cancel my meeting, stay inside and read, rather than spending time with people. I remembered the vow I'd made to myself when I decided to live in Misty Vale. *To walk outside my front door once a day and not hide myself like a hermit.*

"I'll take you for a walk later," I told Sprinkles before I left my cottage. As I locked the door I noticed my elderly neighbour, Margo. She sat in her favourite spot, under the shade of one of her tall trees. I waved. Margo waved back, her gloved hands full of dirt, as she tidied her beloved flower garden. Her floral shift dress and matched the light scarf around her short grey hair. Her face creased with age, and I suspected her magic also took its toll on her health. I'd seen some of the objects she'd crafted from items others would consider scrap. Useful things from wood or metal, fancy outdoor decorations, birdhouses, pot planters, even mailboxes and wind chimes. She earnt enough from her craft to live independently.

Despite the warm weather I was grateful I'd decided to wear a long-sleeved green shirt made of linen. Linen pants, though a pain to iron, were cooler than jeans. It would take me a while to get used to summer in Australia. The sun beat down on the back of my neck and arms, through the protective material. Even at this early hour, the heat shimmered up from the asphalt road. The walk to Willow Street, the main road through Misty Vale, didn't take long. A route I travelled every day, on foot. Only a few hundred metres and I didn't need a car.

Cathy, the proprietor of The Crafty Owl, waved as I passed by. She arrived in Misty Vale and quickly realised the value in opening a craft shop in a town where residents loved to create. People loved being able to see and touch the items before purchasing. To check the quality, to ask questions, and order bespoke items, was more popular amongst the villagers than shopping online. Cathy's workshops were the perfect opportunity to make friends, learn crafts, and have fun.

The workshops I'd attended had been fun. The challenge was in keeping my emotions calm and relaxed enough to be in a room full of strangers. I'd never suspected that I could make a half decent tote bag, table runner, and beaded bookmark. "I'll call in later," I responded with a smile. "There are a couple of items I'm keen to pick up."

Cathy smiled, "I've got some new kits I think you might like to play around with."

My destination today was another of my favourites, The Milky Bar, the local café owned and run by Jess, who took over from her mother. Jess's speciality was baking. Cute cupcakes, macaroons, sweet and savoury muffins, and speciality cookies. In December Jess experimented with festive flavoured cupcakes. I couldn't decide between the peppermint and the choc orange. The sweet treats proved so popular, Jess kept them on her regular menu.

"Hello Jane," Jess greeted me warmly. I visited most days for a coffee and a cake. Caffeine and yummy treats played a significant role in ensuring I left my house for a walk and human interaction every day. I didn't always eat in, sometimes I took the items home with me. "What will it be today?"

"I'm meeting the members of the Misty Vale Midsummer Moonlight Masquerade committee. I'll have a mocha to start with please."

"Coming right up. I'll bring it over to you. The ladies are over there." Jess indicated a table in the middle of the café.

Four women, in their late thirties, were deep in conversation. The lump in my throat, my anxiety reminding me I didn't know how to talk to people, made it difficult to speak. I nodded my thanks to Jess and made my way to the table. The women seemed so at ease with each other; it took all my will power not to turn around and leave the café.

I couldn't. Not now that I was becoming known as Hazel's granddaughter. If I was to help her return to her leadership role, I had to overcome my emotions. No one was out to get me here. People in Misty Vale knew that magic flowed through their veins and weren't afraid. I wiggled my fingers, consciously willing my magic not to manifest as a freak storm, an electrical short, or worse. With a smile plastered on my face I walked up to the table. "Hello, I'm Jane."

The woman with long brown hair stood and smiled. "Jane, how nice to meet you. I'm Maz, we spoke on the phone. Around the table we have Jazz, Rosie and Shaz. Please, grab that spare chair and join us."

As indicated, I chose a chair at an empty table and placed it between Maz, and the woman introduced as Shaz. On closer inspection Maz's hair was darker than mine, with a peppering of grey starting to show through. She wore it tied back in a navy-coloured bow that matched her dress. Her hands showed signs of hard work. Shaz's deep red hair hung loosely around her shoulders. A slighter build than Maz, her red dress complimented her paler complexion. Jazz's stylish short hair was shockingly blonde. The blonde that came from a bottle. Rosie's hair was a light sandy colour, hanging in cute curls around her face. Jazz and Rosie's eyes were bright blue, Maz and Shaz's eyes were dark brown, with greenish flecks.

"Hazel told us you're new to Misty Vale," Shaz's gentle voice broke me out of my subtle evaluation of the women.

"Yes, that's right. I've been here a few months now." I felt uncomfortable talking about myself to four strangers. It felt even odder to ask them for their life stories. They obviously knew each other. I decided to keep to the topic that brought me to their table. "When is the Midsummer Moonlight Masquerade?"

"January 20, less than two weeks away," Rosie answered. "Tickets are already on sale. We have the catering, the venue and the band booked. You grandmother said you may be able to lend a hand," she paused, waiting for my confirmation.

"More than happy to help, please tell me what I can do," I responded brightly, not sure how I'd be able to assist.

Jazz leant her elbows on the table. I noticed what looked like a bird with a large wingspan and hundreds of feathers tattooed on her arm. A phoenix? "That's great, there's still so much to do," she said breathlessly. "There's decorations, sponsors, prizes, posters, and of course costumes..." her voice trailed off.

Maz laughed nervously, "Don't scare Jane away with the long list of chores. We're well on track, but we can always use an extra pair of hands."

"Is it true you are a spirit elemental?" Rosie asked, her fingers drawing little squiggles on the table.

"I am, though I don't really understand what that means. Hazel is teaching me." I was keen to change the subject. "Is there a significance to the date the Midsummer Moonlight Masquerade is held?"

The woman looked at each other. In the end it was Rosie who spoke. "The date for the ball was decided by the residents of Misty Vale years ago. No one can remember exactly why. It's thought to be the date the first families with magic decided to settle in the valley. Over one hundred and fifty years ago. The first celebration was in a makeshift hall in a barn on one of the families' farms. Over the years the event grew and morphed into the amazing gala that it is today." Rosie laughed self-consciously, "At least that's the blurb in the brochures that are being delivered to households in the village."

"That's the story that's been passed down through the years," Maz agreed. "There are tales of the magic tricks performed at the events, of seances, covens, spells and trickery. Mostly tall stories, though they would have an element of truth."

"Or maybe not," Jazz commented. She looked around the table. "Oh, come on now, we live in a town where at least half the population possess some kind of magical ability. Does anyone here think there hasn't been mischief on these formal occasions?"

I sipped my coffee, watching the four women around the table. I envied their lives, growing up where magic was commonplace and everything seemed possible. They spoke about it, like having abilities was normal. "I'd love to hear the stories someday. I don't suppose anyone's written stories about the magic that happens around the village. I spent my life thinking I was crazy or that something was wrong with me," I added by way of explanation.

Shaz reached her hand across the table and briefly touched mine. "You're home now Jane, or do you prefer Clara?" Her cheeks reddened a little. "It feels like we've known you for ages." She looked at the others at the table.

Before I could respond whether I preferred Jane or Clara, Jess arrived with our morning tea. She held a tray with five mugs and a plate of round biscuits decorated as the phases of the moon. "I couldn't resist showing you one of the sweet treats on the menu for the ball," she said with a smile.

"Oh Jess, they're perfect!" Shaz clapped her hands together.

"I didn't know you were catering the ball, they're so cute, and thanks for the mocha." I smiled at Jess.

Before Jess could answer me, Jazz's mobile beeped the tune of a popular television show. I couldn't quite place it, but it was vaguely familiar. "I'm so sorry ladies, Rosie and I have to go," Jazz looked stricken. I wanted to ask what was wrong, but I didn't know these ladies well enough.

"That's okay," Maz patted Jazz's arm reassuringly. "Why don't we invite Jane to our next meeting, at my place?" As her friends nodded, she turned to me. "We meet once a week at my place, for a cuppa, snacks, and a chat. We play around with our magic too. Nothing scary." She must have seen the horrified look on my face at the thought of using magic for fun.

"Our grandmothers were part of a coven, many years ago. They made potions, cast spells, read cards and told the future," Shaz said, her face lit up as she spoke. "We aren't nearly as scary."

"That sounds nice, the cuppa and a chat part," I laughed, willing the butterflies in my stomach to settle. "You have my number, so text me the details and what you'd like me to bring." My head hurt at the thought of using my magic in front of my new friends.

"Marvellous! Sorry to meet and run," Maz said as the four women collected their drinks. Rosie slipped the moon cookies into a plastic container she pulled from her red leather handbag.

"Go do what you have do. I'll have this and meet my grandmother at the office." Internally I breathed a sigh of relief. I watched as the four women waved to Jess and left the building in a flurry and a flutter. I didn't have a chance to ask what their powers were. I closed my eyes and blinked them open again. Shaz – fire, Maz – earth, Jazz – air, and Rosie – water. I'd have to wait until the next time we meet to confirm my intuition.

Chapter Two

The takeaway mug was nearly empty. I didn't have to meet my grandmother Hazel until 10am. I considered ordering another coffee, and maybe one of the delicious looking strawberry cupcakes. Before I could decide, Jess arrived at the table with exactly the combination I'd been debating.

"I'm sorry your new friends had to leave so soon. I've been meaning to get you to taste test one of my new strawberry shortcake cupcakes. I thought you might like another cuppa to go with it." The smiling café owner placed a mug and plate in front of me.

"You read my mind. I was about to come and order one of these." I took my credit card from the pocket on my mobile case.

Jess waved away my card. With her blonde hair tied up in high pigtails, she looked younger than thirty. I knew her age because she'd offered free cake last week in honour of her special day. "Consider it a thank you, on behalf of the café, for what you did to save the village from that awful Florence and her plans to create a spectacle of our peaceful village."

The week before Christmas Florence Hartly, the president of the book club, had been arrested and sent to gaol for a range of illegal activities including fraud and embezzlement. Together with her daughters and brothers in law she tried to turn Misty Vale into a gaudy tourist attraction. "I was pleased I was able to help Hazel and the police," I responded.

"You were amazing! Not only did you persuade your grandmother to return to her rightful role as head of our council, but you unenchanted the crazy Christmas critters that'd sprung to life around town." Jess patted me on the shoulder.

As I concentrated on not flinching at the unexpected human contact, I felt my cheeks redden at the praise. "I fell in love with the village when I hopped off the bus last year. I would've done what I could to save the village, even if I hadn't met Hazel."

"See, that's exactly why I'm here, plying you with free food and drink. To thank you for your bravery," Jess said warmly, once again waving away my attempt to hand her my card.

As the café owner returned to the counter to serve customers, I realised it was the probably the first time I'd been called brave. My work in law enforcement here and overseas wasn't chasing and catching criminals. I was more of an intelligence practitioner – analysing information, conducting interviews, interrogating documents, anticipating threats and protecting community groups. It's why the private investigator role suited me better. I preferred to work alone, behind the scenes. As my own boss I could pick and choose the jobs I took. Luckily, I found richer clientele drawn to my skillset. The money I saved meant I could retire earlier than most people. My substantial inheritance meant I could pay cash for my little cottage. In my spare time, I now helped authors with their social media marketing.

"Hi Jane, Hazel said I might find you here." I recognised the voice of the handsome, tall policeman as he slid into the seat previously occupied by Maz.

"Good morning, Ned," I said, switching my mind from my work in law enforcement, to the good-looking officer in front of me. Since arriving in Misty Vale, I'd helped Ned with a couple of investigations. About the same age as me, with short dark brown hair and brown eyes, we hit it off from the first time we met. We'd quickly become friends, a fact I was still getting used to. My skin tingled at the connection we shared. During all my time overseas, I could count on one hand the number of people I considered more than mere acquaintances. "Do you want to join me? I can get you a cuppa and a cake."

"Thanks, I've already ordered something," he said with a grin. "I can't stay long, but I wanted to have a chat." I couldn't read Ned's expression. We'd been getting together for a meal a couple of times a week. I didn't want that to end. My voice stuck in my throat. Before I could say anything, Ned continued, "I've been advised that Brad and David Hartly have returned to town and are planning to set up some businesses locally."

My spider senses immediately went to full alert. "Did you tell Hazel when you spoke to her?"

Ned glanced at his notebook, then back at me. "No," he admittedly sheepishly. "I kind of hoped you'd tell her. I'll come with you, if you like," he added, feeling bad for leaving me to tell my grandmother the disturbing news. "At the moment I don't know that there's anything illegal about their proposal."

"It can't be a coincidence that they're here, not even a month after Florence and her daughters ended up in gaol. Do you know any details? Exactly what are the Hartly brothers trying to achieve?" I asked. I clenched my fists. A trick I learnt to ease my magic. Whenever I felt anxious, I'd close my hands into a fist. It didn't always stop my erratic powers, but it'd saved embarrassment, and damage to my surroundings, on several occasions.

My handsome policeman friend shook his head. "Not at this stage. There's not much I can do, unless there's a complaint, or they commit a crime."

I understood what Ned was trying to say. "But as I'm not a police officer, I can investigate. I can investigate what they're up to and let you know if there's anything untoward." Although I had decided to retire, there was nothing like a mystery to investigate to get my energy flowing. Crosswords and jigsaws weren't quite the same.

Ned looked relieved. "I hoped you'd say that."

Jess arrived at the table with a takeaway mug and a brown bag of goodies. "I thought you and Sophie could use a snack. Apple and cinnamon muffins," she said as she handed the bag to Ned. Jess turned to me. "I've got a couple of muffins for you and Hazel. When you're ready to go, I'll pop them in a bag for you." Jess returned to the counter before either of us could comment.

After Ned left, I sat a while longer, pondering my next move. A couple of older women I didn't recognise walked into the café. Both sported fancy summery dresses and high heels. "Do you think Brad and David will be successful?" The taller of the two asked as they lined up to order.

"Of course they will. People here will jump at the chance to grow their businesses." I found myself clenching my fists as the women surveyed the occupants of the cafe. I studied the pattern on my coffee mug, straining my ears to hear more of the conversation. "With Robbie's international connections they'll run rings around the residents of this sleepy little village."

"Harrumph," the sound escaped my mouth before I could stop it. Neither woman heard nor glanced my way. They ceased their discussion, as it was their turn to order. After collecting their takeaways, they left the café. I considered following them, but once I exited the building, I decided not to. It was 10am and I was due to meet my grandmother.

Hazel sat behind her desk in our new office. Her green-grey eyes smiled as I entered the room. "How was the meeting?"

"They seemed nice," I thought back to the short interaction. "It wasn't a long catch up. Not long after I sat down, they received a phone call. Something important from what I could tell, they left soon after." I placed the takeaway tray on Hazel's table. "A latte and muffins from Jess." I took one of the muffins to my desk and opened my laptop. "I also saw Ned." I didn't know how Hazel would take the news that the Hartly brothers had returned to Misty Vale. I considered stalling, telling her later. In the end I decided to approach it, like pulling off a band-aid. "He mentioned that Brad and David Hartly have returned to town. They've plans to set up some new business venture. Ned doesn't know the details," I added hastily, taking a deep breath. "But I'm going to look into it, to see what's going on." I knew my grandmother wouldn't be happy with the news. I scrolled through the emails in my inbox, looking for a distraction. "So, what's been happening here?"

My grandmother snorted her opinion of Florence's brothers-in-law. It was difficult to believe Hazel was in her eighties. Apart from her long grey hair, which was today tied into a bun on the top of her head, nothing about her gave away her age. "I see what you're doing Jane, trying to distract me from the news of those two imbeciles." Hazel picked up the takeaway cup on her desk. She side-eyed me as she sipped her latte. "I may have been in hibernation for close to forty years, having stepped away from my leadership role when your parents ran off with you, but I kept up with all the goings on. I didn't trust the way Florence took over and bossed everyone around. I never trusted those Hartly boys either."

I gazed at my grandmother in admiration. My parents hadn't told me about Misty Vale, or anything about the magic in my veins. I wasn't sure how I felt about that. "I'm glad I'm here, with you, and that you've decided to return to your leadership role."

Hazel frowned, side-eyeing me she took another sip from the cardboard cup. "Be careful if you go investigating the Hartly brothers. Going up against them will keep you busy for ages. The office may be quiet now, but I expect it will be busier once January turns into February. While it's quiet, I'd like to take the opportunity to meet with the other councillors. Prepare ourselves before it gets busy." Hazel turned back to her laptop screen. "We've a few emails from people wanting to know about applications for pools, pergolas, fences, and a couple of farms wanting to change their farming practices."

My eyes scanned the emails on my screen. "I don't know why, but I expected to see applications for witchy or magic things. Not that I'm sure what that means," I added with a chuckle.

A knock on the office door stopped any further discussion. "Come in," Hazel spoke with the authority that made me glad we were related.

"Hazel, we heard you were back in the land of the living." Two men swaggered into our office. Both wore blue jeans, brown shirts, and over-sized cowboy hats. The air of entitlement that swirled around them almost made me gag.

"Brad and David Hartly, I thought you'd be in gaol." Hazel strode around to greet them. Her action served to prevent them getting too far into our space. I joined her, cursing my anxiety, hoping our visitors couldn't hear my heart beating wildly in my chest. If my grandmother didn't like these men, neither did I.

"Don't be like that Hazel," Brad, the taller of the two, said irritatingly. "We come here to offer you and your granddaughter the chance to get in on the ground level of an exciting opportunity."

Hazel crossed her arms in front of her. "I don't think so."

"Oh, come on," David cajoled. "Like you, we want to see Misty Vale grow and prosper."

Hazel frowned, "No, you want to make a lot of money while pretending to care about the residents of Misty Vale."

The Hartly men grinned at each other but said nothing.

My grandmother wasn't as tall as the two men in front of us. What she lacked in height, she made up for in attitude. It was clear neither man was going to deny her claim. Hazel pointed to the door. "Please leave, now."

Her tone left no room for discussion. She slowly walked towards the men, leaving them no choice but to turn around and move through the doorway. Hazel shut the door as soon as David's heel landed on the hallway floor. "That was satisfying," Hazel said with a smirk.

On impulse, I enveloped her in a big hug.

"What was that for?" she asked when I finally let go.

"For being amazing, and my grandmother," I replied. "How are they not in prison? If Florence and her annoying daughters, Cindy and Mindy ended up convicted of fraud, they should have too."

"That's a good question; it sounds like one my private investigator granddaughter would find an answer to." Hazel's voice sounded chipper, but I sensed her anger at our uninvited visitors. "I'm suddenly hungry. Are you up for a snack? I'll go pick something up while you do some sleuthing," she suggested.

I raised an eyebrow at my grandmother's sudden switch of topic. I did love a good mystery and was more than happy to oblige. "Yes! This I know how to do," I pulled open a new web page and was tapping away on the keys by the time Hazel left the building. It didn't take long to figure out the Brad and David had used their sister-in-law as the scape goat. Florence would be spending ten years in prison for fraud, while they were free to keep conning people, wreaking havoc on our beautiful village. Florence's two daughters, Cindy and Mindy, also received gaol time. According to my search, their sentences were a lot less severe than their mothers. Did their uncles have a hand in that?

I didn't have to look too deeply into the internet to find profiles for Brad and David Hartly. Both qualified as lawyers, and real estate agents. Their names were connected to several large corporations. Why would they bother establishing more businesses here? Misty Vale was a small, out of the way village, not a bustling city.

The Hartly's weren't unlike the people I had to investigate as a private eye. Rather than hiding from publicity, they took every opportunity to be photographed. They adored the public attention and appeared able to bluff their way around any scenario, according to my research. I scrolled through the images on the screen in front of me. Something about one of the men standing with the Hartly's seemed familiar.

"I hope you like chicken salad," Hazel walked through the door with two brown paper bags and two takeaway mugs. She placed two bags and a mug on my desk, taking the rest to hers. "Jess gave us a couple of forks to make it easier to eat our salad. One of us can return them later."

Closing my laptop, I smiled at my grandmother. "Chicken salad sounds perfect, and I see you added something yummy for dessert." I opened both containers, finding a salad in one, and a jam and cream cupcake in the other.

Hazel shrugged. "We need our strength and energy, especially if we have to deal with people like Brad and David."

"Are the Hartly boys gifted with elemental magic?" I asked as I moved my laptop to make room for my lunch. "Is it a magic skill to be able to talk your way into or out of any situation?" My sense was that they had the ability to sway people's thoughts and opinions.

Hazel nodded at me over her takeaway mug. "That is one of their abilities. They use their magic to manipulate people. I knew you were clever, but you're getting the hang of this faster than I could have imagined."

I blushed at my grandmother's praise. "Can we protect ourselves from falling for anything they say? Like you taught me to protect my home from intruders?"

"We can ensure we are protected from their words and actions," Hazel confirmed.

We ate our salads in comfortable silence. I eyed the décor of our office space and made a note to bring in some cutlery and crockery from home. We both kept meaning to bring in some home comforts, and stationery. Apart from our two desks, four chairs and the small square table, the room contained an old-style metal cupboard that ran the length of one wall under the window. "We could bring in a filing cabinet and maybe a bookshelf, along with the stationery and cutlery," I suggested once my salad bowl was empty.

"Not a bad idea. We can get our office space comfortable before the year gets too busy," Hazel acknowledged. "Did you find out anything interesting about the Hartly's?" She asked as she opened the bag containing her cupcake.

Eyeing my cupcake, I opened my laptop. "They're both qualified lawyers and real estate agents. They own various corporations in Australia, have an interest in several more overseas, and they love photo opportunities." I ran my eyes over the information on the screen. "Instinct tells me their motives are money, money, money. I'm not sure why they think that starting more businesses in Misty Vale would bring in any huge amounts of money. Our village is small, out of the way..."

"Are you okay?" My grandmother asked as I stopped speaking.

"Sorry, yes, there are a heap of photographs of the Hartly brothers in various social settings. There's a man in some of the photographs that I thought looked familiar. He reminds me of an individual I investigated over in England. A nasty little man who was so full of his own importance." I shook my head slowly. "It couldn't be Roberto though, there'd be no reason for him to be in Australia, not with all the business interests he has overseas." I dismissed the idea. "It feels like we need to be wary of the Hartly's. Maybe I'm overthinking it, but does their interest in our village have something to do with that fact many residents are gifted?" I wondered aloud as I stood, stretching my arms.

Hazel looked at me over her takeaway mug. "Let's not waste too much time talking about the Hartly brothers. Tell me about the women you met this morning. What do your instincts tell you?"

"They were guarded, friendly, but I got the impression they were interviewing me before deciding whether to let me in." I still had trouble believing in my ability to make friends. Past experiences had coloured my views on friendship.

Hazel's eyes pierced mine. "You can't use the book club ladies as a benchmark."

"That may be true. My lack of skills with people began long before I met Florence and her cronies. Now that you're helping me learn how to control my magic..."

I never got to finish my sentence, that maybe my people skills would improve as I mastered my magic. Hazel's phone started buzzing. "Hello Hazel speaking. I'm sorry, what did you say? We'll be right there."

Chapter Three

"The hide of those two!" Hazel strode off so quickly, I'd trouble keeping up. It was difficult to believe my grandmother was nearly twice my age.

"The street seems more crowded than usual," I commented we followed a group heading in the same direction.

"Harrumph," was Hazel's only comment. Despite my asking, Hazel hadn't elaborated on the caller or the topic of the conversation. Whatever our destination, it appeared others were headed in the same direction.

In the roundabout where a giant Christmas tree appeared a few weeks ago, a cameraman and reporter stood. I recognised the pair immediately. Barbara and Nicholas were the team who'd reported on the Christmas chaos. The reporter dressed in what I suspected was her trademark bright pink fitted dress and high heels. I wondered if anyone called her Barbie. Nicholas wore black dress pants and a short-sleeved pale blue shirt. He stood behind his camera and microphone ensemble. They faced a group of three men. Dressed alike in jeans, brown shirts, and oversized cowboy hats. I did a double take as I recognised the man standing with the Hartly men. An annoying bully of a man I'd investigated for a well-known security organisation in the United Kingdom.

I nudged Hazel's arm as we pulled up behind the crowd that was rapidly forming around the roundabout. "That man is evil. I don't mean in a magical sense, though he may be magic. I investigated Roberto Patri, and he didn't like me uncovering his deep dark secrets. He threatened me with all sorts of ramifications, for alerting the police to his underhanded business dealings. I'm surprised he didn't end up in gaol. I wonder why he's here, in Misty Vale?" A sense of dread washed over me, as I consciously tried to remove myself from his line of sight. We didn't have to wait long to find the answer to my question.

Barbara shoved her microphone in the space between her and the slightly taller brother Brad. "What can you tell me about your plans for Misty Vale?"

Brad stuck his chest out, thrust his shoulders back and placed his hands on his waist. "My brother David and I used to live in Misty Vale. We have fond memories of the place and its residents, and we want to see the village flourish and grow. We've been blessed with business acumen, and own substantial business interests nationally. We're happy to have been given the opportunity to team up with Robbie Banks." With a grandiose arm gesture, he motioned to the man I knew as Roberto Patri. "Robbie has grown his business from a small mum and dad venture in the UK, to an international success. When Robbie was looking to expand Banks Entertainment into Australia, David and I managed to convince him that as well as looking at the big cities like Sydney, Melbourne, or Brisbane, he should consider other options."

A subdued chorus of 'ohs' and 'ahs' rippled through the crowd. I grabbed Hazel's arm, realised my grip was far too tight, and loosened it. My toes curled as best they could in my black shoes. I had an ominous feeling about this. Hazel must've agreed with me, she patted my arm reassuringly. Her touch served to calm the elemental magic that coursed through my veins. The last thing I wanted to do was draw attention to myself.

Barbara stuck the microphone in front of Roberto, err, Robbie Banks. "How did Brad and David come to convince you that this sleepy little village would be the best place to set up your business?" I cringed at the reporter's use of the words 'sleepy little' to describe Misty Vale.

Roberto wasn't as tall as Brad or David, but he was wider. He puffed himself up as best he could and took a step toward the microphone. "As soon as they confided in me about the special abilities of some of the residents in this quaint village, I knew it was the perfect Australian home for Banks Entertainment," he leered at the reporter, his smarmy smile aimed at the camera behind her.

I wanted to punch Roberto in the nose. As a couple of dark grey clouds rolled overhead, I took a deep breath. I didn't want to cause a storm, although maybe it would scare Roberto away. It wasn't fair on our residents, who were still gathering around the spectacle. The rain would cool things down, but the resulting humidity would be sticky and overbearing. Hazel tapped her fingers on my arm. I felt my pent-up anger energy releasing harmlessly through my fingertips.

"According to my research Banks Entertainment showcases every type of creative skill – artists, acrobats, magicians, dancers, singers, and others. Why would that be something you'd want to bring here?" The condescending tone of the reporter's voice made me want to scream. Barbara knew nothing of our village, save what she learnt during the Christmas chaos. I glanced at my grandmother, assuring her I wouldn't attack the reporter, though the idea of sending her expensive equipment haywire was tempting.

This time David stepped towards the reporter. "Our plan is in its infancy. We'd prefer not to say until we have planning permission and a blueprint to show the details. At that time, we'll make our plans available to the public."

"Is there anything else you can tell us?" Barbara leant forward conspiratorially. "It's not only the residents gathered here," she waved her arm around to include the crowd of locals. "You have a wider audience, who are sitting in their lounge chairs, wondering why you are keen to set up here."

Brad smiled like the cat who swallowed the cream. "All in good time my dear. I assure you. You'll get the exclusive story when we are ready to unveil our proposal." He pointed to where Hazel and I stood at the back of the crowd. "We'll be talking to Hazel and her granddaughter, Jane, in the next couple of days. To ensure a smooth development application process."

I felt Hazel's body tense. This time I patted her arm, to stop her sending Brad tumbling backwards into the road. The image clearly popped into my mind. I must be getting better at reading thoughts and emotions. Barbara took one look at the stony face of my grandmother, and my look of fury, and turned to face the camera herself. Having been on the receiving end of our displeasure a few weeks ago, and she wouldn't have been keen on a repeat performance. "So, there you have it," she spoke earnestly into the camera Nicholas held. "We will keep you updated as soon as the Hartly's reveal more about their plans for this magical place."

"The nerve of them!" I couldn't keep quiet any longer. Hazel led me a couple of steps away from the group of residents. A few heads turned towards me. I recognised Maz and Shaz and smiled apologetically. I lowered my voice and continued, "That Roberto, or Robbie as he calls himself, is some piece of work. I don't much like Brad or David either."

"Neither do I granddaughter. I think in the light of this, spectacle, I need to block out the rest of the afternoon." She frowned in the direction of where the reporter was deep in conversation with Brad. "I suspect this is going to cause us an awful lot of work and unnecessary bother. I want to check a few things before it does. Let's close the office for the rest of the day. I'll lock up. It looks like the Midsummer Moonlight Masquerade committee are trying to attract your attention."

Waving my hand in the direction of the women, I felt the familiar lump in my throat as I thought about the trouble Roberto could cause for the town. The Hartly's seemed to be trouble too. "Are you sure you don't need my help?" I asked.

With a reassuringly pat on my arm, Hazel responded, "Go and have some fun with people your own age. There'll be time for strategic planning later, after I gather some information."

Chapter Four

The Milky Bar was crowded, but Jess led the five of us to a table at the back of the room. "I'll bring coffees and cakes over, I've some new flavours you can test out for me," she said with a smile. As we settled into our seats, I observed the other people in the room. Judging by the buzzing around me, most of the occupants had witnessed the show at the roundabout. I sighed with relief that those responsible hadn't joined the crowd in the café. I didn't want to have to face Brad, David or Roberto. My energy dropped at the thought of that confrontation. As I looked around the café, it struck me that I couldn't name any of the residents, though some faces were familiar. I should make more of an effort to get to know the people in the village I'd chosen as my home.

"What do we all think about the idea of new businesses in Misty Vale?" Maz asked, glancing around the table.

"I think it depends on the business and the types of visitors they will attract," Shaz said thoughtfully.

"The more the merrier I say," Jazz responded, scrolling through some images on her mobile.

Rosie shrugged. "I guess it'd be okay, I haven't thought about it."

"I like Misty Vale as it is," I began cautiously, once I realised the four women were watching me expectantly, waiting for me to comment. "It's a place where people aren't afraid to use their magic. Before I found myself in Misty Vale, I'd spent most of my life running away from my magic. I didn't understand it. I focused on my job and ignored my magic. In Misty Vale I'm becoming comfortable with that part of me." I looked over Jazz's shoulder where Jess's assistant, who looked surprisingly like a tall thin elf, was helping her plate up some cakes. "I wouldn't want any business to change how safe Misty Vale feels."

Maz patted my arm sympathetically. "It must have been horrible, growing up without learning about your magic."

I nodded. "I tend not to talk about it. I didn't understand my magic, and I ran away each time a person teased me about it. My powers cause things to go haywire. Electrical appliances refuse to work, expensive vases shatter, I even caused freak weather events. By products of my anxiety." I glanced at the four women seated around the table at The Milky Bar café with me.

It was an uncomfortable feeling, baring my true self, leaving myself open to criticism by these ladies. But I trusted my grandmother. She told me this group of women could be trusted. My instincts weren't so sure. I put that down to my trust issues and nervousness around new people. Roberto in Misty Vale rattled me.

Jess arrived at the table with a smile and a tray of mugs and plates of small cupcakes. "Here are some new treats to sample. We have moonlight mocha mud cake, chocolate raspberry, and silky strawberry cream cake. If you like them, I'll make some for the ball."

"Thank you," my voice added to the chorus of the other four at the table.

The bell above the door jangled as five people entered. I groaned inwardly, when I realised the only free table was the one close to us. Brad and David Harty, and their friend swaggered over to the table and noisily pulled the chairs out. Barbara and Nicholas hurried after them, squashing themselves in the space in between the businessmen.

I turned so I faced away from Roberto and the others as best I could. Concentrating on my food and drink I let the sweet hazelnut latte flavoured drink trickle over my taste buds. Taking a bite from the mocha cupcake, the burst of bittersweet flavour made me happy. Maybe everything would turn out okay after all.

"Jane? It is you, isn't it? Jane Fairweather!" Brad Hartly leant over and grabbed my hand, shaking it rigorously, not giving me a chance to refuse.

"Brad, David," I nodded curtly. I debated acknowledging Roberto and the reporters. Barbara was too busy leaning forward trying to engage Roberto in conversation. Nicholas stared at the table in front of him, wishing himself anywhere else.

"Brad, David, you know these lovely ladies? Please introduce us." I did my best not to gag as Roberto stood and with his hand outstretched.

"Certainly, Robbie Banks, please meet Maz, Jane, Shaz, Jazz, and Rosie. Members of our annual masquerade ball, and Jane is also a member of our local council." Brad introduced us to his business partner.

"It's lovely to meet you ladies," Robbie Banks moved to our table, shaking each of our hands in turn. Before I could decide whether to call him Roberto and have that conversation there in the crowded café, Jess arrived at their table with their order. Probably for the better, I didn't want to make a spectacle of myself or cause a magical incident. My fingers reached for a second cupcake, chocolate raspberry this time. With real raspberries and chocolate chips. Sweet, but not overbearingly so.

"You're quiet Jane, are you okay?" Shaz asked gently as she placed her coffee mug on the table.

"Sorry, I zoned out there for a while, thinking of all the things I still have to do today." I didn't want to mention my concerns about the Hartly's plan to grow new businesses on town, or that I knew Robbie Banks by another name. I did my best to change the subject. "You ladies look like you've been exercising," I said, indicating their change of clothes. They wore oversized t-shirts over black leggings, instead of the summery outfits they wore when we'd met earlier.

"Yoga," Rosie replied. "In the community centre. Until we heard about the news broadcast."

"News travels quickly in the village," Jazz added.

"How did you end up in Misty Vale? If you don't mind me asking," asked Shaz as she picked up her mug once more.

"I don't mind, though it feels odd talking about myself." I sipped my latte. "I returned home, to Australia, after years in the UK. I decided I wanted to see more of the country, and I hopped on a coach. When the bus stopped here, something about the village intrigued me. I decided to stay a little while. I found a cute cottage for sale and chose to stay."

"Did you know your grandmother lived here? Do you have other family?" Jazz asked.

"My parents are both dead. As far as I knew, I had no other family. I'm still getting used to having a grandmother, and possibly other family." I wasn't keen on talking about myself with the Hartly's and Roberto nearby. "Enough about me, fill me in on what I need to know about our lovely village. What are the key benefits to living here?"

"Oh, my goodness, there's so much, I wouldn't know where to start," said Shaz. She turned to Maz. "Maz knows everyone, she's involved in so many committees."

Maz laughed off her friend's compliment. "I do know a little about the village, and the old magic that entwines through generations of families."

"Lately there's been an increase of magic being used openly," Rosie added.

Jazz looked up from her mug of hot chocolate. "That's okay, as long as people are using magic wisely, and not trying to harm each other."

This wasn't news to me. Ned and I had talked about how people seemed more comfortable using their magic in public, since the Christmas chaos. But I didn't want to discuss it with Brad and the others nearby. "It's probably something the council will talk about next time they meet," I suggested. Hazel had briefed me on the workings of the council, which comprised magically gifted and non-magical residents. The monthly agenda included ordinary agenda items, and issues related to the magic in our community.

"I'm pleased Hazel decided to take on her council role, and that you're helping her," Shaz murmured.

"Speaking of which, I should probably be getting back to work," I fibbed. My anxiety was improving, but I was beginning to feel claustrophobic. The number of people in the café, the proximity of Roberto at the table, the reporters, and even my new friends. I needed an escape. Saying my goodbyes, I promised to catch up with the ladies again soon.

"Jane, it was lovely to meet you." Robbie, aka Roberto's smile made my stomach turn. He stood, blocking my way, his eyes revealed he recognised me too.

"Robbie, Brad, David, Barbara, Nicholas," my heart pounded as I spoke curtly, pushing gently past Robbie. He stepped back, letting me past.

With no particular destination in mind, I chose to walk the long way home. The community centre sat in the front section of the local park. On the side of the building a carpark area had been repurposed to accommodate the weekly craft markets. Many of our residents created useful or ornamental items, showcasing our villagers' abilities. I made a note to walk through the next market, to check out the local crafts, gourmet foods, and magical items.

"Hello Jane, I came by the office to have a chat, after the spectacle at the roundabout, but you weren't there. The office was closed, is everything all right?" Ned, the first friend I made when I landed in the village, exited the door of the police station. My eyes lit up as the tall handsome man with dark brown hair and matching-coloured eyes joined me.

I felt my cheeks redden. I was still getting used to the mutual attraction and blossoming friendship.

"After we heard what Brad had to say, Hazel had some errands to run, and I ended up having a cuppa with the masquerade committee,"

I replied, resisting the urge to touch Ned's arm. He wore his uniform, and I didn't want to be the cause of gossip. "I think Hazel is seeking legal advice regarding the business opportunities the Hartly's are proposing."

"I think it's wise to be prepared, when it comes to Brad and David," he cautioned. "If I finish my shift on time, I was thinking we could catch up for a chat, or a cuppa."

"It sounds good. I'm heading home now, call in whenever you get a chance," I replied. Ned lived in the granny flat at the back of the police station. It made sense to meet at the café, or my cottage. He loved spending time with my pets, and they enjoyed his company. We said our goodbyes, and I kept walking the few hundred metres to my front door.

Chapter Five

I swung my head around, as I heard a faint cackling sound behind me. Nothing looked out of place. I was only a few houses from home. The houses along the street were of weatherboard or brick construction. Most properties were fenced, their front yards containing established trees and shrubs. It was probably a bird calling its mate. As I stepped forward on my way towards my cottage I heard it again. A faint cackle, a little louder than an evening breeze. I expected to see a wizened, crooked old crone, standing over a cauldron, the sound was so real. In the months I'd lived in Misty Vale, this was the only time I'd heard such a noise.

Sprinkles met me at the front gate, his tail wagging, ecstatic at my arrival. "Hey little guy, you can't hear any old witch cackling, can you? It must be my imagination." I dismissed the noise, as I unlocked the door and went inside. At first, I didn't notice anything out of place. While I'd not brought a lot with me when I moved, I'd collected bits and pieces in the six months after my arrival.

Sprinkles followed at my heels as I headed for the kitchen. Cinnamon wandered over from her cushion. "Are you joining me in case I have food for you?" I asked bending to pat both my pets. Animals were so much simpler than people. I scratched the top of my pup's head and stroked my cat's back. Bert chirped his greeting. "And good afternoon to you too," I smiled at my feathered friend.

Once the animals were happily munching their food, I set the kettle to boil. That was when I noticed a couple of the kitchen cupboards were open. Two of the drawers too. I closed them, "Did I leave in that much of a hurry this morning?" I asked my menagerie, wishing they could talk in a language I understood. "Probably nothing to worry about," I added as I scooped a generous serving of coffee into my mug.

I gasped, when a visit to my snug revealed open drawers in the tallboy, and my basket of wool knocked over. "I guess we've had a visitor," I told Sprinkles, who'd joined me and sniffed around the wool that had escaped the basket. "Do you know who did this?" Neither of my furry friends appeared stressed. Did that mean they knew the visitor? That didn't bear thinking about. A check of my bedroom revealed the same level of mess. As I put items where they belonged, I mentally checked off a list. Was anything stolen?

The only jewellery I owned, I wore. The emerald on my ring glowed fiercely. One of five stones that represented each of the elements, the ring connected to my powers in a way I was only beginning to understand. The only other item of sentimental value was the shoebox that contained a few memories of my childhood. It sat in the bottom drawer of the tallboy, exactly where I left it. I exhaled in relief.

My hand flew to my mouth as I realised which items were missing. The antique key and wooden box that were somehow connected to my powers. They'd found me around the time of the Christmas chaos. "Where did I put them?" I asked an uninterested Cinnamon. "I thought they were in here, oh hang on," I rose to my feet and headed back into my bedroom.

For Christmas, Hazel had given me an old woollen shawl that used to belong to her mother. Made of fine silvery-purple wool that shone in the moonlight, its powers were linked to mine. I lifted it out from under my spare sheet set. "Thank goodness!" I exclaimed aloud, unwrapping the shawl to reveal the box and the key where I'd placed them at Christmas time. Instinctively I knew these magical items were what the intruder was looking for.

"What about my metal box?" I exclaimed, kicking myself that I hadn't hidden it with the other items. Cinnamon rubbed against my legs, meowing. "What is it?" I asked her. My cat walked over to the upturned basket. She started pawing at the strands of wool sticking out underneath. I joined her. As I lifted it, the basket felt heavier than I expected. In the bottom of the basket, tucked in between the woven straw, was my metal trinket box. I reached in, dislodging it from its hiding place and checked it over for damage. I looked at Cinnamon admiringly. "How on earth did you do that? You hid it from whoever came in here." Cinnamon responded by sitting beside the wool, preening herself.

A cold wet nose sniffed the box and my hand that clutched it. "Let's see if I can remember the protection spell Grandma taught me," I told my pup. I debated ringing her, but I wasn't sure how long her errands would be, and they'd sounded important. Invoking the enchantment at each entry point to my cottage, I drew the protection symbol, the stones of the ring glowing brightly as I did. A sense of calm washed over me. Did that mean the spell worked? I took a breath, exhaling slowly as I looked around.

Although the evidence showed an intruder, it didn't feel like my space had been invaded. "How does that work?" I asked aloud. Cinnamon wrapped herself around my legs. "It's a shame you're not my familiar, or maybe you are." I sank to the floor, letting her climb into my lap and snuggle in the space made by my legs. I'd been reading on the internet about witches who had familiars. Animals who were both companions and helpers, assisting in magical practices, even providing guidance and protection.

Sprinkles sat quietly on the floor in the kitchen where I'd plonked myself, watching me stroke Cinnamon's back. Normally he'd be vying for attention. "I found you in my back garden under the bushes," I whispered to Cinnamon. "I assumed you came with the property, like Bert." Sprinkles had followed me home and quickly become a member of the family. "If you're my familiar, did you find me, rather than the other way around?" I felt a little silly with this line of conversation. The blue stone on my ring shone more brightly than the other crystals. The tiny blue stone on my cat's collar twinkled at me. "Okay then, what if I suppose you are my familiar," Cinnamon's eyes, a similar deep cinnamon colour to her fur, stared intently into mine as I spoke. "You could tell me if we are safe here, if a thief broke in or if the mess was the result of a scrying spell chanted somewhere else."

Cinnamon stretched and nudged my chin. "Does that mean my intuition is correct? I suppose we should work out a system. Rubbing my chin for yes, what symbol means no?" My cat turned so her tail flicked me in the face. I laughed out loud. "Either I'm going crazy, or I've figured out how to communicate with my cat."

Sprinkles tapped my knee with his paw. "Are you magically inclined too?" I glanced up at my budgie. "Not you too?" I asked incredulously. Bert chirped, hitting his bell with the top of his head. Sprinkles stood, chased his tail and lie back at my side. I laughed out loud. "Okay, okay, so you are all my magical helpers. So, help me out, let me know if my intuition is correct."

Three pairs of eyes stared intently at me.

"They were looking for this metal box." I held the delicate piece artefact in the palm of my hand. "They didn't break in physically, they used a crystal ball to spy in my cottage, to find and steal this." I watched my pets, who were watching me. I stood slowly. "They were searching for the key too, weren't they?" Cinnamon responded by walking across the hallway to my bedroom. She jumped up onto my bed, her paw on the shawl near the key. Sprinkles followed me. I considered opening Bert's cage so he could join me, but I wasn't sure it was a sensible idea. "An image flashed in front of me. "You guys caused the chaos, to confuse the scryer, so they couldn't find what they were looking for, thank you, you clever creatures." I patted Sprinkles and Cinnamon.

Before I'd a chance to process what happened, my mobile beeped a cheesy Christmas tune. "Hello Hazel." I moved back into the kitchen, reheating the water in the kettle. "Were your errands successful?" I'd no idea where my grandmother had disappeared to. My guess it was related to the public display of macho earlier.

"It went well, nothing for you to worry about. How was your afternoon tea?" I heard the curiosity in her tone.

My coffee at the café seemed like such a long time ago. "It was okay, until Brad and co arrived." I poured some milk into my mug. "It was what happened afterwards that made it more interesting."

"I see," my grandmother paused, "and pray, do tell, what happened?" I pictured her face, her brow furrowed, as she enquired about my afternoon.

"Someone rifled through my belongings. Intuition tells me they did so remotely, and that they were looking for my key, and the metal trinket box. Also, I can't believe I'm saying this, but I think that Cinnamon may be my familiar. Sprinkles and Bert too." I gulped a couple of mouthfuls of my coffee, waiting for a response from my grandmother.

I pictured her half smile as she spoke. "I wondered how long it would take you to work out that Cinnamon and the others found you, and not the other way around."

"I suppose Esmerelda is your familiar?" I asked. Hazel's large grey fluffy tabby rarely left her side when she was at home.

"She is. Tell me about what happened at your cottage," Hazel asked quietly. "Do you need me to come over? Did you call Ned?"

I smiled at my grandmother's concern. "Thank you, but I'm okay. I think whoever was scrying for my treasures got confused when my pets created a mess. Though it looked ransacked, nothing was taken. Is it possible for magical beings to burgle remotely?"

"It is," my grandmother conceded. "Any of the magical families in the village have members who know how to look through walls, across

streets, to find things. You could perform the same type of enchantment."

I snorted, quietly. The idea that I could scry for something in the
next room, let alone across town sounded doubtful, if not impossible.
"I'll have to try that one day." I said in jest, though I could see the merit
in the skill if I was still working as a private investigator. "I've set a protection spell, using the ring, and Cinnamon approves." I glanced at my
familiar, licking her front paws, the nodding motion of her head confirming my thoughts. "I can't remember, why did you ring?" My brain
was buzzing with the array of things I could achieve with my magical
abilities. For the first time in a long time, I felt my gift could be an asset
as well as a curse.

"I wanted to check in to see how your afternoon tea went. I knew
something was off, but I couldn't figure out what. It must have been
Brad and the others at the café. If you're sure you don't need me to come
over, I'm going to have an early night. I suspect we're in for a busy week.
We'll meet first thing tomorrow, put our heads together, and figure this
out."

Hazel's intuition was spot on. The arrival of Brad and the others
had un-nerved me. As I shared my story with the masquerade committee, I sensed the women were hiding something from me. Which made
no sense, as the four had been nothing but friendly during both meetings. I shook my head to clear my thoughts. "I'm overreacting, aren't I?"
I asked Cinnamon. She turned until she faced away from me. Did that
mean no, she thought my intuition was correct? Was I crazy, taking my
cues from the actions of a domestic cat?

Trust yourself.

I spun around, the whispering clear enough that I expected to find
someone sitting next to me. I glanced at my pets. They returned my
gaze. I needed to trust my own intuition if I planned to assist the
committee, work with Hazel, and deal with Roberto and the Hartly's.
Roberto, or Robbie. He'd made it clear in the UK, that he wasn't im-

pressed I'd advised the authorities of his behaviour, and that I'd pay for that.

Trust your magic.

This time I saw a flash of light on the edge of my vision. I turned towards the back door as a shadowy figure disappeared through the closed door. Before I had time to investigate the apparition, there was a loud knock at my front door.

Chapter Six

Ned, still in his uniform, stood on my doorstep. A welcome distraction from unwanted house guests, ghostly visions, and underhanded business dealings. My energy buzzed, excited at seeing my friend. "I'm so pleased you could make it; I'll put the kettle on." I followed Ned into the kitchen as Sprinkles yapped excitedly around his legs.

"I'm sorry, I hoped to be here earlier, it got a little crazy this afternoon." He stepped to one side as Sprinkles jumped up at his leg, tail wagging eagerly. "Hey there fella." Ned bent to pat the dog's head.

The policeman knelt to roll the ball for my pup as I clicked the kettle on for the third time since returning home. "Anything you can tell me about?" I scooped coffee into two deep blue mugs, hoping for a practical puzzle I could help solve.

Ned brushed his hand across his forehead as he sank into one of the wooden chairs at the kitchen table. "There appears to be an increase in magic occurrences in town. Similar to what happened at Christmas. A large body of water appeared in one of the streets on the outskirts of town. Residents are making use of it as they would any other swimming hole in this weather. Another street has been turned into a giant slippery slide, complete with showers of water. I know it's hot weather and school holidays, but parents aren't normally this free with their magic." Ned referred to his notebook. "There are a few ice cream trucks with wizards and witches handing out free ice creams."

"At least none of that sounds menacing," I said, placing the mugs on the table. My stomach gurgled as I remembered the muffins I'd made the previous evening. I plated up a couple of apple cinnamon muffins with a handful of berries and grapes.

"True, but menacing or not, the occurrences are keeping Sophie and I busy. We must answer each call-out and ensure the safety of the townsfolk. She's young, but Sophie takes no nonsense from anyone. She manages crowd control better than any cop I worked with in the city." He reached for a muffin. "Thanks for this Jane, I won't be able to stay long, but this is exactly what I needed.

Holding his gaze as we both sipped from our mugs, I sensed he referred to the company, not the coffee and late afternoon snack. "I'll put together a lunchbox of food for you and Sophie. As much as I'd like you to stay for longer, it would be horrible if you didn't attend a call out and it ended up being something mischievous, or dangerous," I agreed. Cinnamon rubbed her side along my legs. Not keen to take her for granted now I realised the connection between us. I wanted to tell Ned about the ransacking, and about that pompous twit Roberto. That there was something underhanded about Brad and David.

"What do you think about Brad and David's proposal, to bring new businesses into Misty Vale?" Ned asked. I was almost certain my policeman friend couldn't read my mind.

"The television interview caused quite the commotion," I began, "I don't like the Hartly's or their friend. That reporter too, she's annoying."

Ned chuckled, "I love how you always tell it like it is." He reached his hand out, briefly touching mine. "I've heard varying opinions. Some residents are outraged at the idea of more business changing our little village into a tourist hot spot, while others are hoping to ride on the back of the success of the venture and start their own business. I'll be honest, if I didn't love my job, I'd consider having a go at a small business."

This surprised me. I'd not considered Ned as anything other than a law enforcement officer. "What type of business would you like to run?"

"Something outdoorsy, maybe hiking, taking customers to local places of interest. Or a woodworking workshop. I've always wanted to learn and teach woodwork. I don't think I have any specific skills, but I learn quickly and I'm good with people. My grandpa used to let me help in his shed. He made toys and bits and pieces out of wood for his neighbours, family and friends. Maybe I'd run the run the scenic walks a couple of days a week, and the woodworking on different days." He chuckled. "Right now, though, I'm happy with my job. Policing in a village is so much nicer than in the big city." Having worked in the police force in big cities and small, across several countries, I knew what he meant. "What about you? If you could run any type of business, what would it be?"

I thought about Ned's question. "I enjoyed my job as a private investigator, on most days. I like helping authors with their editing and social media. I'm not sure what help I'll be to Hazel on council, and I can't think of anything else I can do," I answered honestly. "Investigation and puzzle solving isn't exactly a skill that's highly sought after, in a village this size. Unless you are the local policeman." I grinned.

Ned eyed me over his coffee mug. "I think you'd be surprised, people are nosy, sticky beaks by nature. You'd probably be inundated with customers, although I suspect helping Hazel will be a fulltime job, especially with the Hartly men's business dealings. I'm curious, did you use your powers in your cases?" He popped a couple of berries into his mouth as I considered my answer.

"Not knowingly. I used the internet, and I asked a lot of questions." Blending into the shadows, watching the subject of the investigation suited me. I wasn't a fan of confrontation. "It would've made my job easier, if I'd tuned into my intuition and instinct. The trickiest part, as it would be with your job too, is establishing the facts from the fiction.

Examining each minute detail to prove or disprove theories." I questioned everything, doubted everyone until I was able to establish the truth of the scenario. My tenacity and dedication resulted in lifelong gratitude from some powerful people. Lifelong enemies from equally powerful, disgruntled people. Roberto being one of the latter.

Full of nervous energy I returned to the kitchen. I retrieved two slices of caramel slice from the fridge and added them to the plate on the table. Choosing a large plastic container with a lid, I filled it with slice, muffins, a couple of bananas and apples.

"What do you think of the Banks Entertainment idea?" Ned asked as he picked a piece of caramel slice.

"Absolutely rubbish. I don't trust Mr Banks or the Hartly's one iota." I felt my cheeks reddened as the anger I felt towards the proposal flared. As Ned uttered the words Banks Entertainment a vision flashed in front of me. Something between a circus and an academy teaching the craft of magic the scene so real I had to blink several times to clear it.

Cinnamon nudged my ankle. I bent to stroke her fur. Sprinkles placed himself at Ned's feet, staring at the policeman with wide brown puppy dog eyes. "There's something I need to tell you," I began. Ned deserved to know what I did about the three businessmen. "I know Robbie Banks, as Roberto Patri, a con man with disreputable business investments. He wasn't happy when I provided the evidence of his dealings to his wife. He stole large sums of money from her, and other investors. A security company, headed by his wife, commissioned me to investigate his business and personal activities. He threatened me, that I'd pay for my actions. This was a couple of years ago, in England. I assumed he'd still be in gaol. Misty Vale is the last place I expected to find him." A wave of anxiety ran the length of my spine at the thought of having to face off against Roberto. Of all the subjects I'd investigated, he'd been the most challenging.

"Did he give any indication that he knew or recognised you?" I heard the concern in Ned's voice.

"Apart from the layer of smugness and arrogance that oozes from him, when he had an audience, he pretended not to know me. He wouldn't want the Hartly's and the community to know about his past. At the café, his mask slipped for a second. He recognised me." I shuddered at the memory of his eyes staring at me as I left the table. "I don't trust Brad and David either. I did some research on their qualifications and businesses. They may even know about their new business partner's past indiscretions."

Ned reached for my hand and gently squeezed it. "I can see that Robbie, er, Roberto's presence has upset you. I can't interfere unless a crime has been committed, but I'll ask Sophie to perform a background check on Robbie Banks, and Roberto Patri." Ned scribbled in his notebook. I loved that like me, he preferred to use old fashioned pen and paper, in place of an electronic tablet. "Brad and David are almost locals, though not all our residents will be keen for new businesses in town." His eyes met mine. "What are you going to do?"

I mulled over the question. What was I going to do? "I'll talk to Hazel, and I'll conduct my own research, but other than that, I'll wait and see what happens before I make a fuss. I'm committed to Misty Vale. It's home. You're here, and Hazel, and my animal menagerie. I might finally be over running away from my problems," my voice wavered as I Ned caught my gaze. His fingers caressed the back on my hand.

Ned's mobile beeped, breaking the moment. I chose a piece of slice, as he scrolled through the message. "I have to go," he sighed as he pushed his chair back, reluctantly eyeing the plate of food. "Someone has commandeered the showground, has set up a huge screen, and is giving out popcorn, ice creams, hotdogs and lollies. So many of our residents are heading there that it's caused a minor traffic jam."

"It sounds like a promotional stunt for Banks Entertainment." I handed him the container of food I'd prepared. "There's enough in there for you and Sophie." I walked towards the door with Ned. "I'd not be surprised if the Hartlys were also behind the ad hoc pools and ice cream trucks. Their powers are as questionable as their work and ethics."

"What about Roberto, does he have magic?" Ned asked.

I cringed, what a horrible thought. "Not that I'm aware of. He's revolting enough, without adding powers to it. Be careful," I added as Ned made his way to his car.

"Roberto was one of those cases where justice was never served. His multi-million-dollar business in stolen antiques was hidden behind a legitimate family-owned airline. He smuggled the rare artefacts himself. Piloting small planes to sneak in, steal priceless items and sell them on to other less than reputable antique dealers. Roberto's wife employed me to check up on him. She thought he was having an affair. The security company she owned suffered financially, not because of an affair. He was embezzling money as well, from many of their combined business concerns." I paused, as my mind ran through the details of my investigation. "Officially Roberto was based in Gatwick, and ferried freight and passengers back and forth between Europe and the United Kingdom. A deep dive of his finances showed an enormous fortune. My research confirmed him a bully and a narcissist. His wife wasn't much better. Once I provided evidence that he was unfaithful and trading in stolen goods, his wife Carol, paid me, advising my services were no longer required, and demanded I not go to the authorities with my findings." Telling Hazel all about Roberto, aka Robbie Banks, was exhausting. I leant back in my knitting chair.

After a short pause, my grandmother asked a question, her voice strong as it travelled through the phone line, "Why do you think he is here? Did he seek you out, or is this coincidence?"

"My instinct is he that was surprised to see me, that he didn't plan on coming here to cause me grief. If that had been his goal he would have called me out the first chance he got. My gut tells me that he's waiting to see what I'll do. I suspect he simply met the Hartly brothers on one of their overseas jaunts, or maybe at a conference, and saw an opportunity to make a huge amount of money at the expense of others." I sipped my peppermint tea, glad I'd decided to ring Hazel and update her, before we met the next day. I'd a feeling we both needed to be ready for whatever happened next.

I moved into a more comfortable position as I heard my grandmother's voice. "The Hartly's will be striving to get as many residents on side as possible. Free treats are a sneaky, clever way of getting locals to listen to them. Offering help to establish businesses is clever. They'll be making a profit on any locals who sign up. We'll have to careful how we tread. We can't refuse their development applications without assessing them honestly, or we'll be made out to be the baddies," my grandmother mused.

"I was thinking similar. We'll need to make notes, to be able to argue the point, if we're challenged on any decisions." I agreed. My anxiety rose like indigestion in my throat.

"There's nothing we can do now. Tomorrow we'll plan a way forward." Hazel's voice calmed me. "We'll have a big few days ahead of us, let's try and get a good night's sleep."

As I slept, a large group of disgruntled locals chased me out of town for revealing Roberto to be a criminal mastermind. As I stood at the edge of town, where the t-intersection offered the road into the city or our village, I flung my arms in the air. The movement caused a large crack in the ground to open up and swallow Misty Vale. I woke with a jolt. My sheets saturated in sweat that had nothing to do with the summer heat.

Chapter Seven

My mobile assured me it was 4am and there was no news of any village swallowing incident or damage to Misty Vale. With Barbara and Nicholas camped out here, it would be all over the news if I or anyone had caused the village to disappear. Unless I'd unwittingly made them disappear too. Now that was an idea.

I sat up against my pillows as Sprinkles and Cinnamon eyed me from their positions curled up on my bed. I must've kicked a lot, as the blankets lay askew, half covering them. In that in-between daze where my dream felt nearly as real as my bed, I closed my eyes. I was immediately transported back to the spot at the end of town, at the edge of the forest. Except the town was gone. Strange noises came from the forest beyond me. Cautiously I stepped around the forest debris, following a path that appeared to be lit by hundreds of tiny creatures. I squinted at the humanlike figures whose whole body glowed and shimmered, lighting my way.

The noise grew louder. Eventually I reached a clearing. In front of me, a scene from a circus unfolded. Instead of clowns, young wizards in capes, brandishing wands were practicing a comedy routine. Cupcakes flew through the air as they waved their wands. Streams of lollies danced around the wizards. The beep-beep of the clown car introduced a small van into the clearing. The young wizard in the back of the van handed out ice creams to the children trailing behind the van.

I blinked, in the dream, and found myself in the middle of the village. Where the roundabout used to be, a large slippery dip stretched along the main street. A long hose attached to sprinkler heads engulfed the area in water. Roberto, dressed in a circus ringmaster's outfit stood in the middle of the street, directing traffic.

When I opened my eyes again, I couldn't see anything. I felt around the room, as my eyes adjusted to the dark. The floors and walls around me were made of rough lengths of wood, like a log cabin. Muffled voices came from the next room. A beam of light snuck under the door from the room beyond. I recognised the voices immediately.

"Hazel ran and hid last time her life got a little tough. All we need to do, is blast her with work, questions and challenges. She'll run and we can lead the village," Brad's voice carried through the gaps in the construction of the building. I fumed but held my temper in check. Even in a dream I wasn't sure that my magic wouldn't cause damage.

"Jane's not such a pushover," Roberto's voice rang out clear as a bell. "Like a terrier with a ball, she won't let go."

"Maybe she's more like her grandmother than you realise," Brad suggested, oozing arrogance.

"Or she'll get angry if we send her grandmother away. You did say Jane and Hazel possess magic powers, are we likely to be in danger?" Roberto wasn't dumb, he was trying to assess how much of a threat we were.

"I wouldn't stress about their powers, Hazel's old, and from what I can tell, Jane wasn't taught how to use hers. Don't worry, I don't assess either as threats to our plans." Brad's voice told me he thought the conversation was over.

I strained my ears to hear more of the conversation, but it was as if the volume had been switched off. When I opened my eyes, I was back in my bed. Sprinkles lay draped over my feet, Cinnamon lay across my lap. "Were you making sure I didn't vanish?" I asked as a yawn escaped. Cinnamon nudged my chin.

By the time I typed up as many of the details as I could remember, the sun shone through my kitchen window. "Breakfast time," I told my eager menagerie, measuring food into the three bowls. I showered quickly while they ate. Although it was going to be a scorcher, I opted for black pants and a light mauve shirt. I needed to project a professional appearance.

Hazel knocked on the door at 7am sharp. "Let's grab breakfast at the café, before we head to the office," she said, bending to scratch each of my pets behind their ears.

"Be good today," I patted Sprinkles, "And look after them," I whispered to Cinnamon. Waving goodbye to Bert, I crossed my fingers that the protection I set yesterday would hold.

I climbed into the passenger side of my grandmother's older style olive green jeep. The trip to The Milky Bar café was one I normally walked. It made sense to drive when we had a full day at the office ahead. Banksia Street, where I lived, was one block back from Willow Street, the main road through the village. A route I walked each morning. Today it felt different. There were more people than normal milling around the café door, and the roundabout, where a large sign had appeared overnight.

"What a monstrosity!" Hazel snorted in disgust. The poster, the size of a billboard, advertised Banks Entertainment and Hartly Brothers Business-to-Business Services. Along with the words, ginormous head shots of their smiling faces blared out for all to see.

I shuddered at the sight. My dream felt more premonition than crazy nightmare, though it could have been a little bit of both. "We can stop this, right? They can't just come in here and set up businesses, can they?" Did villages like Misty Vale operate the same way as the bigger cities? Hopefully there was a layer of rigor around new businesses.

"We should be able to, unless they get most of the townsfolk behind their scheme. It would be more difficult to stop them then." Hazel pulled her jeep in an empty spot behind our office building.

"This is unusually busy for early morning, even in the school holidays," I commented, noticing the cars already parked around us.

We exited the jeep and followed a family of five out of the carpark onto the main street. "Is there really a circus coming to town today?" The girl with blonde pigtails asked her father.

"A circus?" I looked at my grandmother.

"Yes!" The older boy, with sandy coloured hair, turned around, a big smile on his face. "Those men," he pointed to the faces on the billboard. "They said on television, that they were bringing a circus to town. A different circus than normal, this one will have wizards and witches."

"And ice cream," his little sister said excitedly.

I bit my tongue. Otherwise, I knew I'd swear, and I didn't want to upset the family or the others heading in the same direction. I wiggled my fingers gently, letting my energy escape without causing any damage to my surroundings.

"That sounds like a fun day," I heard my grandmother say. The main street was even busier than when we drove past a few minutes earlier. "Typical," Hazel muttered under her breath. The shop next to the café, that once housed Hartly Real Estate Agents according to the sign, was open. A poster advertising the circus hung in the window.

Two women, similar in age to me, sat at an outdoor setting outside the office. Both women wore bright pink fitted dresses. The lady with her long dark hair tied in a high ponytail handed out envelopes to passersby. The blonde, with her hair loose around her face called out "Be at the showground at noon today, for an afternoon of fun, free food and entry into the circus."

"Cindy and Mindy," I muttered. "I thought they were in gaol."

"Their uncles got them released. Their mother Florence has been left to take the blame for the events in December." Ned walked up behind us. "Can I interest you ladies in a coffee before work?"

I linked arms with Ned and my grandmother, not caring who was around to gossip. "You certainly can. We were on our way to the café ourselves, and we're not the only ones." My heart sank at the number of customers lining up at the door to The Milky Bar.

Hazel squeezed my hand. "It's not that crowded, and we'll get a feel for what people are thinking about the goings on in the village."

Grandma was right, I sighed and held my head up as we walked through the door into the café. "Not all these people are locals," Hazel commented as we waited in line.

"Visitors and tourists aren't necessarily a bad thing," I began.

"Except when it is because of the Hartly's," my grandmother finished my sentence.

"It's a strange choice of a place to be initiating big business plans," Ned agreed.

The young elvin creatures who assisted Jess at the café were busily making coffees and handing out pastries and muffins. "The twin teens look so much like their grandparents," Hazel commented. The youngsters were tall, thin, with long blonde hair, pale skin and pointy ears.

"They do, don't they?" Jess said with a smile as we arrived at the counter. "Kat and Kit have been a godsend. When it's quiet in here, they bake delicious treats and create new recipes. It's like having a bunch of magic helpers," she giggled. "What would you like today?"

"Three large caramel lattes," Hazel suggested.

"How about half a dozen assorted pastries, you choose which ones, and a couple of cupcakes for Ned to take and share with Sophie." I added.

"And a large mocha for Sophie please," Ned finished.

Hazel glanced around the room, buzzing with activity. "We'll take ours as takeaways please. It's a little busy in here this morning, we'll head to our office."

A cold shiver ran down my spine. I turned to Ned. "You mentioned yesterday that you needed to talk to us."

Ned nodded. "I did. I still do. Not now though, we've been called out to a few incidents this morning already. Why don't Sophie and I bring lunch, around midday, to the office and we can chat."

I glanced at Hazel. She gave me a thumbs up symbol. "Perfect, we'll see you then," I responded, as Jess's helpers handed us our orders.

Exiting the café, we parted ways. Ned headed to the station, and we made our way to the office. A large crowd was forming at the table outside the estate agents. Barbara and Nicholas were in the midst of the group. I groaned, "Not another live telecast."

Hazel steered me away. "We can watch it later. I'm sure they'll post a video on social media. They want the people to watch and become involved. It's all about getting carried away with the hype. Whether we love it or hate it, it's all publicity to them."

As my hands were full with our takeaway mugs, I wiggled my toes, willing my pent-up energy to move harmlessly out into the atmosphere. I counted my breaths in and out, as we passed by the group of chatty locals. A woman I didn't recognise, dressed as a fairy, was handing out cupcakes to excited children. I frowned. "How dare they! Jess's trademark is her amazing cupcakes."

"Careful," my grandmother warned, as the cake stand full of sparkling treats threatened to topple as I vented my feelings.

"Can't I at least enchant the cakes, so they taste like cough medicine, instead of sugar?" I whispered.

Hazel winked as she clicked the fingers on her hand that wasn't carrying our breakfast. "Not medicine, toothpaste." We quickened our pace, moving away so we couldn't be blamed when children started spitting their treats out in disgust. We were opening the front door to the old switchboard building when we heard the first moans of protest from some of our younger citizens.

Chapter Eight

It was less than an hour later, after we'd finished our breakfast and coffees, that the emails began to arrive. Our computers were configured so we could both see everything pertaining to council matters. I don't know what I expected, but it wasn't to be inundated with development applications. I counted ten different applications as I printed two copies for us to read through. Old school, I preferred to be able to scribble on the document. I suspected my grandmother was the same.

"More visitors in town does benefit our local businesses and artisan crafters," I acknowledged, trying to see the positive side as I handed copies to Hazel. "Although I didn't expect so many applications," My anxiety manifested as a nagging sick feeling in the pit of my stomach. I returned to my desk and started reading the applications.

"It's not a surprise that the Hartly's and Robbie Banks have submitted applications for Bank Entertainment," I heard anger in Hazel's tone. "The area they propose to develop is too close to the main shops for my liking." She sighed, "But they do own the land. The Hartly's bought up a lot of property a few years ago."

I looked up from the document I was reading. "So that makes it more difficult for the council to refuse the application?" I asked.

Frowning down her nose, Hazel replied, "Yes, it'll probably come down to whether the general public have any problems or reasons not to build an entertainment centre there."

I scanned the documentation. "Hartly's want to build a magic academy on the other side of the entertainment centre." I held up the second application from the real estate agents.

"Hah," Hazel sounded cranky, "And the other application, from Robbie, to develop the old warehouse at the end of Fern Street, into a supermarket that sells magical items for the discerning wizard and witch."

"Even the name, the Magician's Den, sounds pretentious," I agreed. "At least some of the other applications are from locals. Speciality shops for homemade local crafts, arts and artisan foods stuff. The sort of thing Misty Vale is already known for."

Hazel opened an empty manilla folder on her desk and slid the emails into it. "We'll have to meet as a council and talk about which proposals to seriously consider, if we can deny any, and pros and cons for each. Not in that order," she commented with a wry smile.

Before either of us could start on a list for the meeting, the office door opened. Brad, David, and Roberto strode in. Hazel and I stood, to protest the intrusion. Brad waved his hand, dismissing whatever we were about to say. "Why don't you both sit and listen to for a moment."

"I'll stand," Hazel spoke firmly. I stood my ground, across from my grandmother as we both faced the intruders.

Brad shrugged, "Suit yourselves. You would've seen the applications for the businesses we want to develop in and around Misty Vale. Will the businesses make us a lot of money? Sure, but an increase in business opportunities in the village makes sense for our residents and the local economy." His steely eyes held my gaze, then Grandma's, before we each turned our heads away. "We're here to discuss how we can help you. I'm sure you both have ideas for your own businesses. Why don't we talk about how we can assist you with your dreams?"

Hazel stepped around her desk until she stood close to Brad. She wasn't nearly as tall as the ex-footballer, but still formidable compared to anyone. "Why don't you leave my office and never return," she countered.

David stepped towards me. "What about you, Jane? Do you have a business idea you'd like to develop? Didn't I hear you were a private investigator or a policewoman? We could set you up in competition with the local plods. I hear you'd run rings around them."

"Out! Now!" I stepped towards the three men and pointed towards the door. I walked slowly until they had no choice but to back out through the open doorway. As I closed the door behind them, Roberto, the last one to leave, turned around and sneered at me.

I drew in a deep breath and exhaled. "Well, that was revolting," screwed my face as I turned around.

"I agree," Hazel said, returning to her desk and opening her laptop. "We have our work cut out for us if we are to rid our village of those three, before it goes so far that it's too late to stop them."

As I forced myself to calm the energy racing around my body. I remembered our conversation yesterday afternoon. "Did your appointment go well?"

"Yes." She shuffled the printed copies of the applications. "We need to tread carefully, but we should be able to save our town from this nonsense." From her serious tone of voice, I knew she'd not stop until we found a way to prevent the three men from changing the village. I also knew there was no point in asking more questions about her mysterious appointment. "Let's prepare for a council meeting as soon as possible."

When a gentle knock at the door interrupted our planning for the second time, I sprung around my desk, ready to give whoever was on the other side of the door a piece of my mind.

Ned and Sophie stood in the doorway, their arms full of takeaway containers from Jess's café. I replaced my frown with a smile. "Come in, let me set up the table in the middle of the room."

"Whoa, I'm glad we're not the people you expected to see on the other side of the door," Ned quipped.

"We're always happy to see you both," Hazel commented, bringing two chairs around to where I'd dragged out the side table.

A couple of minutes later, the four of us were seated around the small side table. "We bought some chicken burgers, chips and some macaroons for dessert," Sophie said as she unpacked the food.

"Iced coffees as well," Ned added.

"Thank you, both of you," Hazel's voice was softer than earlier, but there was still a hint of her determination to protect the village. "It's just what we need, after our earlier visitors."

"Brad, David, and Roberto," I explained. "They underestimated our ethics and thought they'd entice us with their offer to start our own businesses."

Ned eyed me and Hazel. "There's no right answer to that statement," he chuckled.

Sophie looked at me over our lunch. "Ned mentioned you thought Robbie Banks may be worth investigating. You were right." She pulled her tablet out of the jacket pocket. "He doesn't exist as Robbie Banks until a couple of years ago. Around the same time as Roberto Patri disappeared. A lot of their personal details differ, but their fingerprints are the same. Both used fingerprint and voice recognition in their security protocols. There were enough similarities in their business practices to raise red flags. How he's escaped prison time I'm not sure. There's no evidence either personality possesses magic."

I leant my elbows on the table. "I thought the same. None of my research uncovered any evidence of Roberto having magic. He's a ruthless businessman. He's got millions of dollars he obtained criminally, and he has a knack of staying out of gaol."

"I fear that his partnership with the Hartly boys will provide him more protection from law enforcement," Hazel agreed.

"Gee, what revolting mealtime conversation," I laughed. "Can we please enjoy the good food and the great company? Problems are better solved on a full stomach." However Jess and her helpers created their food, there was a magic imbued in each mouthful. None of the café food was greasy, or high in salt or sugar. The burgers were crisp, with fresh tomato and lettuce, cheese and a sweet chilli sauce. We ate in companionable silence.

"Is there anything you need from us?" Sophie asked. "Not that we can do anything officially unless they break the law."

"Thanks, but as you say, they haven't broken any laws yet. We'll have to deal with each application on merit, and with the help of the other council members. If we require police involvement, we'll let you know." I turned to Ned, "Didn't you say you needed to talk to us about something?"

Ned wiped his hands with his napkin and sucked iced coffee through the oversized paper straw. "Remember I told you about the incidents, the pools, lollies, and ice creams magicked around the village to tempt people? I'm almost certain it's a clever ploy of Brad's to win over the villagers." Without waiting for a reply he continued, "That being said, some of the locals appear to be using their magic more blatantly than before. Which isn't a problem itself. Residents are free to use their powers, as long as they don't hurt anyone. I'm worried that with Barbara and Nicholas here filming and conducting interviews, we'll become news for all the wrong reasons." He looked from me to Hazel and back again. "I guess I hoped one of you might have an idea of how to lessen the impact, or something..." his voice trailed off.

"It's tricky," Hazel said over the top of her drink. "We can't dictate what people can and can't do. Apart from 'do no harm,' and 'nothing dangerous,' we are all free to use our magic. Traditionally most of us chose to contain our magic to the privacy of our own homes. I'm happy to bring it up at the council meeting, to see if the others have any ideas."

Ned rubbed his forehead. "Thanks Hazel." He glanced at Sophie, as she scrolled through her tablet. "I guess we'd better go," he added reluctantly.

"I'm afraid so, there's reports of individuals setting off fireworks. I'm sure that even magic fireworks are a fire hazard in the middle of the day during summer," Sophie said as she helped me move the table back to the side of the room.

"Thanks for lunch," I smiled as they left the room. I took the rubbish outside and left the door open when I returned. "This way we can see people coming," I explained with a grin.

The next hour we spent in silence. Each time I glanced at Hazel I saw her scribbling on her notepad. I fluctuated between reading the applications, making notes and trying to find something, anything incriminating on the internet. Roberto, Brad, and David covered their tracks well.

Grandma broke the silence. "Why don't we invite all the applicants to come and talk with us? A formal interview process. If they're serious about setting up a business, they should be willing to talk through the details." Hazel suggested.

"That would be a good way to get to know them, their motivations, and more about their business ideas. Would we have to afford the ringleaders the same opportunity?" I asked, observing my mentor.

"Probably." Hazel sounded as impressed as I at that thought.

My intuition nagged at me. There was something about the applications we were missing. I scrolled back through the printed pages. Listening to my intuition was a skill I'd paid attention to only since arriving in Misty Vale and finding Hazel. If I'd used my intuition years ago, my life may have been quite different.

"Every decision and step along the way led you here, to me, now," Hazel read my mind. Mindreading was another skill I'd inherited, and I wasn't entirely comfortable with this ability. It felt like an invasion of privacy. "Maybe it will come in handy as we try to wade through the applications," Hazel again broke into my thoughts. "Reading minds, and our intuition I mean. I agree, my intuition is telling me we're missing something. Let's go through the details, make notes, and plan our approach."

I stared around the room, looking for, I don't know what, inspiration of some kind. My brain was looking for a clue. It felty like I was missing an important piece of information. "Maybe I'll go for a walk, and practise mind reading." I stretched. "I might even figure out what my intuition is trying to tell me."

Hazel's fingers fiddled with the tiger's eye crystal she wore on a gold chain around her neck. "I can't believe that neither of us thought to use the ability to read minds when Florence and her daughters caused so much trouble last year," My grandmother spoke softly. "Use your ring to pay attention with people and events around you. The more you use your skills, the stronger you'll be. While you're out I'll arrange the meeting with the councillors. I'll map out a list of potential times for interviews with the applicants too."

My initial concerns that Hazel may struggle with the task of once again being involved as a leader in the village were unfounded. Grandma didn't need babysitting, and I enjoyed spending time with her, we worked well together.

Even with the increased foot and vehicle traffic on the main street, getting out into the fresh air made me smile. It was replaced by a frown as I observed Brad, David and Roberto. Chatting to people, like politicians canvassing the streets for voters.

Until I met Hazel and learnt she was my grandma, I was happy with my quiet, hermit like existence. During the Christmas chaos I was a curiosity – as Hazel's long-lost granddaughter, Clara Thorne. As I watched the conversations in the street, I realised something. As Hazel's relative, I could no longer hide in the shadows. As Jane Fairweather, or Clara Thorne, my role was to stand up to the likes of these men. It didn't matter the name I took; it was about how I conducted myself. If people were to understand who I was and what I stood for, I needed to know myself.

The people listening to, or chatting to Brad and the others were normal, average citizens. A young woman pushing a pram, an older couple strolling with their walkers, a couple of middle-aged women dressed in polo shirts advertising their businesses. Did I recognise their faces? I couldn't be sure. If they were interested in what the businessmen had to say, then I'd make more of an effort to get to know them. I just wasn't sure how.

I glanced at my hands. Ordinary, plain Jane hands. Hands that could start a fire, or a flood, or cause an electrical storm. My fingers could manipulate a keyboard and find information about people, knit a toy reindeer, make caramel slice, and plant an herb garden. As I zoned in on my hands I heard whispers. The young woman was anxious about her children at school, and whether she was a good parent. The old man winced as a shooting pain ran down his back. He was worried what would happen to his wife if he died first. She was concerned about the pain her husband was in, and whether there was a miracle cure. The short haired woman advertising her beauty business was curious as to how Brad could help grow her business. The woman with the pink polo shirt wondered if she could get a job at the new entertainment centre.

Without trying to, I even managed a glimpse into Brad's thoughts, before he blocked me. His glee at having so many people interested in their proposal was unsettling. David was easier. He was counting dollars and planning a trip overseas. At least he wasn't aiming to staying here once the business was up and running. Roberto was as sleezy in his thoughts as he appeared on the outside. I turned away before I inadvertently stumbled on his intentions.

I wanted to help Hazel protect the village from evil doers. I enjoyed solving problems, puzzles and mysteries. Maybe the key to my making a difference, supporting Hazel and the village, was my magic.

Slowing my pace, as I passed the shops, I watched the ad hoc gatherings. The auras of the three businessmen were murky. No surprise there. Most of the residents appeared genuinely interested and concerned about the future of our village.

My instincts wandered, seeing the shopfronts as if for the first time. A hardware store, a chemist, a newsagent, a general clothing store and a toy shop sat alongside the craft shop, the real estate agents, and the café. I counted five empty shops. There were others stores, down the side street. I made a note to check the internet and see exactly how many local shops were in Misty Vale. The next closest town was a twenty-minute drive away. The city at least an hour's drive. Having a variety of successful family businesses in the village could be a good thing.

As I passed the real estate agents, I noticed a group of people talking to Cindy and Mindy. Two men and two women, dressed in business attire. I didn't recognise them, and their auras where tricky to read. The six were learning forward, speaking animatedly. Outsiders wanting to establish businesses in the village. I caught random words – restaurant, winery, equine centre, training. I dawdled, hoping to eavesdrop, and learn more. Mindy glared at me. Reluctantly I kept moving.

Where were Barbara and Nicholas? I walked along the side of the park, passing the police station, hoping to catch sight of my friendly policeman. Animated voices in the middle of the park drew me in. A small pink caravan dressed up like a gypsy van sat in the middle of the park, near the play equipment. Children and their parents lined up for free ice creams. A wizard dressed in a grey robe and pointy hat handed out ice cream cones to the children. Barbara held her microphone, whilst Nicholas angled his camera towards the scene.

At the back of the line of excited children, an older smartly dressed man waved his walking stick. "You shouldn't be here! Giving out free ice cream, bribing children and their parents. You should be ashamed of yourselves!" He swung around towards Barbara and Nicholas. "You shouldn't be filming it; you're only encouraging them."

Sophie headed towards the man with the stick, while parents moved their children out of the line to a safe distance. "Come on Mr

Henry," she steered the man to one side. "Let's go have a cup of tea and a chat." Mr Henry frowned at the gypsy van, but he let the policewoman lead him away.

Barbara walked over to me, shoving her microphone into my face. "Clara, or should I call you Jane? You're Hazel's granddaughter. What are her views on the plans for the businesses in town? What are yours? Do you both support what Brad, David, and Robbie are trying to achieve?"

When the reporter finally drew a breath, I responded, "Good afternoon, Barbara, thank you for asking such pertinent questions. Hazel and I are working our way through the development applications we received this morning. Once we've read them, we'll talk to the applicants. What happens from there is up to the council and the village. I trust you'll be respectful of the process. There is a balance between reporting the news and ensuring privacy. I'm surprised you're still in Misty Vale. I hope you're enjoying your holiday in our village."

Barbara was as surprised by my diplomacy as I. I'd not planned what I said, the words tumbled out of my mouth before I'd time to check them. "Thank you for your honesty, Clara," she replied, before turning her microphone back to the parents and children gathered around the pink van.

Rather than stand around watching the wizard hand out ice creams, I returned to the office, walking through the car park to the back door, to avoid the main street. I wasn't keen on seeing Roberto and the others again.

"I'm thinking about changing my name to Clara," I blurted out as I opened the inner door to our office.

Hazel looked over the top of her computer. "Oh, yes? And why is that?"

I drank from the water bottle on my desk. "It's who I am, especially now, in Misty Vale. My name doesn't matter as much as what it stands for. Clara Thorne. Your granddaughter. A woman who's learning her magic. Someone who cares about what happens to this town."

Hazel smiled knowingly. "I knew you'd be strong. Stronger than your parents who ran away instead of challenging the rules so they could marry and bring you up in a home surrounded by family. Stronger than I, who hid away when your parents' left town. I should have chased after them and brought you all home." She wrapped her arms around me and hugged tight. "You're more courageous than I. You're a true leader and you'll make sure our village stays safe. One comment I'll make is that your name doesn't make you who you are, it's who you are inside that makes the difference."

I gulped my fear away. Not wearing the role of a leader easily, I wanted to protest, that I wasn't cut out for the role. But a tingling in the middle of my forehead told me she spoke the truth. I opened my mouth, but no words came out.

Hazel held me at arm's length. "I see your worry. Concern that you're not cut out for this, yet your intuition tells you otherwise. Trust yourself." She squeezed my hand before returning to her desk. "While you were out, I spoke to the council members. We're meeting tomorrow morning. I've emailed you a draft agenda and a list of the development applications."

Chapter Nine

A salad with walnuts, leafy greens, crunchy noodles, diced chicken, grated cheese, tiny tomatoes, and a plate of buttered fresh bread stick. "Thanks Jane, after a day running around after incidents that turned out to be advertising tricks, this is the perfect meal," Ned said, as he piled his plate with salad, adding a couple of pieces of crusty bread.

"It's a pleasure," I felt my cheeks redden. "Roberto cornered me at the supermarket. If I wasn't starving and didn't want food here in case you called in, I would've walked out without any groceries."

The handsome policeman placed his hand on mine. My pulse quickened as our skin touched, sending tingles rippling through my body. "I'm pleased you suffered through Roberto's annoyance, this food is good, and the company is amazing." He took his hand back so he could continue eating dinner. "What did he want?"

The bread tasted so good, I must've needed the carbs after such an emotionally exhausting day. "Roberto, told me, in a snarky whisper, that if I knew what was good for me and Hazel, I shouldn't broadcast what I know about him." I sipped some water from the tall glass in front of me. "I wasn't sure whether I'd go public with what I know about Robbie Banks," I held Ned's gaze.

"And now?"

"And now I'll be making darn sure I have a plan to reveal his true character, when it's appropriate to do so," I laughed nervously. "Let's not talk about annoying people. It's been a long day. Let's just eat dinner and enjoy each other's company."

Ned's eyes twinkled. "Exactly what I was thinking," he grinned. "I have a question, you're a spirit elemental, is that right?" Although he'd lived in Misty Vale most of his life, Ned and his family members didn't possess magical abilities.

"Yes. Apparently being born of two spirit elemental parents makes my power different from anyone else's. It also means I can manipulate the other elements, water, wind, earth, and fire. If I concentrate and my powers don't go haywire," I added.

"It's a shame that when you parents fell in love, it was taboo. If you'd been able to grow up here, surrounded by others, you'd have learnt about your magic." Ned's eyes searched mine as he ate his salad.

My heart leapt at the way he looked at me. "True, but then I wouldn't be who I am, and who knows, maybe we wouldn't have met and become friends. Everything happens for a reason." Cinnamon slinked off her cushion and joined us; her dainty little paws kneaded my feet.

We finished the rest of our meal in companionable silence. Roberto had been so annoying that I'd left the supermarket without picking up items for dessert. I searched my pantry cupboard. "All I can offer is a piece of slice and a muffin. Oh, and there's hot chocolate if you'd like some."

As I boiled the kettle, Ned's mobile beeped. He pushed back his chair, looking longingly at the steaming mug of chocolate.

"Do you have to go right now? Can you drink this first, or should I transfer it into a travel mug?" I opened the cupboard above the kettle to reveal an assortment of mugs. Sprinkles joined Ned, tail wagging excitedly, hoping for a walk.

"Not tonight, Sprinkles," he patted the pup on the head. "A travel mug would be awesome, if you don't mind. Sophie's been swamped with calls about more magical incidents." He shook his head as he scanned the screen of his mobile. "Apparently Brad and co are being interviewed by Barbara in half an hour. Something about a solution to the worrying increase in the use of magic powers." He wiped his brow and tucked his phone back into his pocket.

I poured the contents of both mugs into travel cups. "I'm coming too." I glanced at Ned. "If you don't mind." Without waiting for an answer, I bent to pat Sprinkles, and Cinnamon. "I won't be long. The protection should keep you safe. Bye Bert." I picked up both cups as I followed the policeman out the door.

Ned opened the passenger door. "I suppose you'd better hop in," he gave a wry smile. "Sophie will meet us there."

Before I had a chance to ask where 'there' was, a bunch of fireworks burst out in the evening sky. The brilliant white, red, and yellow lights were followed by smaller bursts of blue and green sparks. "Fireworks, more pools springing up in local streets, pun not intended, gingerbread houses, caravans giving away ice creams and lollies, giant slippery dips, there's even a street with carnival rides and show bags," Ned muttered as we drove past some of the larger events. "I can't arrest residents for using their magic. They're not harming anyone or breaking any laws as far as I can tell," he sighed as we passed a once empty block that now contained a fairy castle. The structure stood as tall as the plastic play equipment in the local park. Made of bright pink bricks, with two small purple dragons standing guard in front of the castle. Small flying creatures that looked like I imagined fairies to be, flitted around the dozens of children squealing in delight. Their parents stood to one side talking in hushed tones.

"The sky isn't usually this dark in the early evening in the middle of summer," I commented.

"Hmm, more magic, I guess," Ned answered, as he swerved to avoid a couple of gnomelike figures on the road. Luckily, the nearly full moon, and the glow from the fireworks, mean it was easy to see where we were going. We drove past a group of teenagers in the school grounds, conjuring fireworks using branches as magic wands.

"I can't begin to imagine experiencing this as a kid. I'm sure as a teen I'd have gone a little crazy testing my powers," I mused aloud.

Ned glanced at me, before returning to face the road, turning left in time to miss the pool of water forming in the intersection. "It's a little like what's happening all around the village at the moment." It couldn't be fun, being the police in a place where random magic could cause chaos, injury, or worse.

I craned my neck to see the magically created swimming hole. "What's that shimmering light around it? Maybe a security measure to stop people falling in."

"Clever," the policeman said grudgingly. He turned the car into a cul-de-sac. A short normally quiet street. Tonight, it was full of people.

Three life sized gingerbread homes stood along the road. People milled around, children squealed excitedly, as women dressed as witches handed out baskets of sweets and chocolates. "I guess if the parents are okay with children having sugar filled treats this late in the day, it's not a crime," I quipped.

Ned sighed. "You're right. The same logic applies to the giant slippery dips and the carnival road. Until there's an actual crime, there's nothing we can do. We turn up and keep an eye on things. People need to know we're here if they need us. We'll head to the roundabout and listen to the interview. I'll need to help Sophie with crowd control."

Moments later, he swung his car into a space in the car park behind the row of shops. I climbed out of the car, surprised at the shiny glitter scattered on the asphalt road. "Thanks for the lift. I can walk home after. It's not far and well lit. You'll probably be busy for a while."

"If I can, I'll drive you home," Ned replied as Sophie waved from the entry to the alley way. Ned quickened his pace to catch up with her. I followed, allowing them space to talk about how they'd handle any issues that came up during the interview.

I sent Hazel a text, letting her know where I was and what was going on. A few seconds later I heard her voice behind me. "Well granddaughter of mine, let's see what they have to say for themselves tonight." She wrapped an arm around me as we joined the others waiting for the interview to begin.

Barbara wore a red dress that made her look like she belonged in a soap opera, rather than a reporter on a news channel. I wondered which man she'd dressed to impress. I found the three entrepreneurs vile and arrogant, but I knew enough about people that many women would have swooned over their rugged looks and confident attitude. The men wore dark blue dress jeans, black shirts, dark brown boots and cowboy hats.

Nicholas set up the camera and sound equipment in the middle of the roundabout. Bright orange cones cordoned off the roads on either side. Sophie had done her best to ensure safety in a village full of magic.

The reporter held her microphone and stared into the camera. "We are here in the little village of Misty Vale, a town known for whimsical, mystical people with crafty skills. You may remember late last year when Christmas characters came to life and created havoc here." She smiled her fake beguiling smile into the camera. "I'd like to introduce you to three men – Brad and David Hartly and Robbie Banks. They've come to Misty Vale with a dream to take this place from a little sleepy village to a place where people will want to visit, to be entertained. Their dream includes a plan for locals to take advantage of the increased tourism, to share their arts and crafts with the world. Brad Hartly, one of the men with a vision for Misty Vale will talk a little about their plans." Barbara stepped nearer to Brad, moving the microphone close to him.

Brad's cheesy smile rivalled the reporter's fake one. "Thank you, Barbara, and thank you for coming to Misty Vale. We appreciate you helping us spread the message about the wonderful opportunities that are available to the residents and visitors who choose to spend time here." He spread his arms to encompass the other two men. "My colleagues and I want to provide a place where people can gather and be entertained. For the creatives in our midst, it'll be a venue for you to display your skills. Banks Entertainment will showcase international, national, and local talent."

David stepped closer to his brother and the microphone. "That's phase one. We're looking to make a significant positive difference. We've set up a trust fund to help individuals establish their own businesses." Where they stood on the grass, a magical light cast an eerie shadow over the group. The men's faces were clear, but everything else was a little fuzzy. I moved my hands a little, turning up the lighting around the whole area, so I could study the scene in front of me.

The aura around the three men was murky. I heard a faint buzzing. "I hear it too," Hazel whispered. "I think it's their aura, trying to mask their true intentions." I squeezed her hand that I understood her words, my eyes never leaving the three men performing for the camera. There was no stage, but it felt like they were actors putting on a show for us.

Roberto leant into the microphone. "We're considering building an academy where people can learn more about their magic. While there's nothing wrong with the impromptu magic displays we've seen around town, we feel it would be a positive to have the opportunity for locals to learn the finer details of their craft." He leered at Barbara with what he probably thought was a charming expression on his face. "The whole village will benefit if those with magic learn better how to control their powers."

I gauged the reaction of the crowd. Most appeared enthralled, happy with the men's proposals. "How condescending can they be!" I whispered loudly to Hazel. She silently squeezed my hand. Were we the only two people not fooled? Were the Hartly brothers somehow controlling the emotions and thoughts of the crowd?

A man around my age raised his arm. "How much is all this going to cost us? Will our rates increase? Our utility bills? What about the costs to go to a show, or attend classes?" A few murmurs in the crowd indicated they agreed with the man's questions.

"All costs for village locals will be heavily subsided by funds from each of our corporations, for the first few years," Brad smiled into the camera. "We want you all to be able to sample the benefits first hand. Share your positive experiences by word of mouth, invite your family and friends to come and check out all that Misty Vale has to offer."

"What if we don't want the village to change? I like it the way it is." An older lady called out.

"Change is inevitable, but we can try our best to ensure a positive experience," Brad added. "Honestly, if we don't think of ways to encourage visitors to our village, local businesses will suffer. These enterprises are aligned with the specific skillsets of our residents." He looked around him. "It's late, and it's been a long day. Why don't we reconvene tomorrow? Join us at the showground and spoil yourself with some of the free food, drink, and entertainment we've made available. Tomorrow and over the coming days, we can discuss the details."

I had to do something. I wasn't going to let Brad take charge of the situation. I squeezed Hazel's hand, dropped it and walked quickly to where they stood around the microphone and camera. "May I?" I asked Barbara. Eyes wide, she pushed the microphone towards me. "Thank you," I acknowledged her, before facing the camera. "Thank you, Brad, David, and Robbie," It took all the self-control I could muster to keep my voice light and neutral. "We appreciate you looking out for the residents of Misty Vale. My name is Clara Thorne, I'm Hazel's granddaughter. Some of you may know me as Jane Fairweather, the only name I knew for the first thirty-plus years of my life. Hazel and I are meeting the other members of the local council tomorrow morning to discuss the business development applications we've received. Then we'll meet with the applicants individually. I'm sure our residents will love the entertainment and refreshments you've planned for tomorrow, just remember there are processes to follow. Our role is to make sure the proposals are a good fit with our current businesses and our community. We will arrange a town meeting, to give residents a chance to provide feedback. Hazel and I are available to chat, on the phone, via email, or call into the office during business hours. Thank you." I smiled at the camera and the people gathered around.

Hazel took both my hands in hers as I returned to her. "Thank you," she whispered. My eyes were on Brad, and Robbie. Were they going to jump back on the microphone, or leave it to Barbara to close the interview?

"You heard it here first folks, stay tuned, it's going to be a busy week in Misty Vale, where the summer weather isn't the only thing heating up," the reporter beamed at the camera as if she was telling an exciting, enchanted tale.

Nicholas packed away the equipment while Barbara huddled with Brad. David tried to walk away from the scene, but three women cornered him. "Are they flirting with him or asking him about business opportunities?" I turned to Hazel, rolling my eyes.

"Probably both," she replied. "They are sisters with magic skills; they own a catering business. They're probably canvassing to cater some of the corporate events. I guess there's nothing wrong with that." I noticed the look of distain on my grandmother's face but refrained from asking about it.

Robbie was surrounded by a group of people I didn't recognise. As I opened my mouth to speak, my grandmother shook her head slightly, indicating she didn't want to speak in the crowd. "Would you like a lift home?"

I glanced over to where Ned and Sophie were busy with traffic control. "That would be lovely, thank you," I responded, giving Ned a wave as we left.

I hopped into the passenger seat stifling a yawn.

"I'll pick you up at seven in the morning, we can have breakfast and prepare for our day," Hazel suggested as she pulled her car up outside my cottage.

Chapter Ten

I unlocked my front door and turned on the light. Sprinkles bounded up to say hello. Cinnamon sedately joined us as I walked through to the kitchen. "Hi guys, I ran into Grandma Hazel when we were out," I chatted to my animal family as I boiled the kettle for a chamomile tea. A tea I'd not tried until Hazel made me a cup after Christmas dinner. A calming tea, she suggested. I now drank chamomile tea before sleep most evenings.

My first Christmas with my grandmother had been memorable, for more reasons than the herbal tea. She'd insisted on all the trimmings. A large roast and vegetables, with Christmas pudding, pavlova, cream, custard and ice cream for dessert. The day included crackers, tinsel, tree decorations, food and lots of presents. I took some slice, cakes and fizzy water with me. We spent a day reminiscing. Hazel told me about my parents and their families. The family I missed out on knowing. As I waded through all the feels – sadness, regret, happiness, joy, disappointment, my energy surged.

"I can teach you how to control that," Hazel commented as she passed me a plate of Christmas pudding and custard. "You've such a raw power, like nothing I've seen before. Your magic is a mix of earth, wind, fire, water, and spirit." She walked around my chair. "I can teach you all I know, but I think, after a couple of weeks, it will be you who teaches me."

Her words made me smile. "That's nice of you to say, but I doubt that." I wasn't normally a fan of fruit puddings, but as I ate the dessert

Hazel gave me, I gained a new appreciation of the food. The rich fruity flavours blended with the rum, cream and ice cream. My energy buzzed and I felt myself becoming more comfortable with myself.

"A couple of weeks later and here I am, calling myself Clara," I told Bert as I gazed around my kitchen. "This place feels like home." I hadn't changed a thing in the country kitchen, apart from adding my large table and dining chairs, their light wood a similar tone to the cupboards and bench tops. I'd bought the basics for cooking and loved trying new recipes. The window overlooked the backyard, which was full of mature trees, shrubs, and the vegetable garden I'd started.

I stared at my hands. Since moving here I'd used them to dig the soil, make slices, knit, and learn other craft skills, and magic. If I concentrated, I could see the rays of coloured lights threaded across between my fingers. Like a mini rainbow. Or fairy lights. I moved my hands towards the grey metal box on the table in front of me. I held my fingers slightly above the box. The lid jiggled, a little. My eyes squinted, as I concentrated on the lights, as Hazel taught me. I forced my face to relax, taking a deep breath in, breathing it out through my mouth. My fingers moved back and forth, over the top of the box. Slowly I moved my fingers away from the table. The box wobbled a little, then rose off the table. I was so shocked I broke the spell and the box clattered back to the table.

Sprinkles yapped excitedly, Bert chirped in his cage. Even Cinnamon looked up from where she was preening herself. "Sorry guys." Maybe I'd practise with a softer item. I walked into my snug. It contained a fireplace I'd not used, and a little window from where I could see the road in front of my house. I'd added a chest of drawers as a sideboard, my cozy armchair, a small television on a side table, and the large basket where I kept all my wool.

I lifted a thick ball of plush pink wool out of the basket. I managed to levitate the wool thirty centimetres above my patchwork chair. When it dropped it didn't make a noise. "I'll take it as a win," I told

Sprinkles. He tried to grab the ball as it fell, but I rescued it before he slobbered all over the wool.

An image of Roberto flashed in my mind. I swung my hand to banish his likeness from my mind. The wool flew across the room and landed on the ledge above my fireplace. Seeing Roberto in Misty Vale, hearing his snide, sneering, yucky voice had been unsettling. "I wanted to close the door on my past and start a new life here. He was the nastiest of those I'd investigated. One of the reasons I left the UK was to distance myself from my old job, the old me." Bert chirped comfortingly as I talked through my fear at coming face to face with one of the people I investigated. "Maybe, if I can master my magic, I can stop whatever Roberto has in mind. At the very least I'll make sure Hazel and I, and you three, are safe." It was late, and I should be in bed, but I wasn't looking forward to the nightmares I knew would chase me once I closed my eyes.

I wandered around the kitchen table. Bert eyed me from his perch, balancing on one leg the way birds do. Cinnamon lay curled up on her pillow in the snug. Sprinkles looked at me. I bent and ruffled his fur. "I know a protection spell, I can levitate things, I think I can read people's minds, and I'm learning more each day." Sprinkles tail wagged back and forth crazily. "Surely, I can manage to sleep without having weird nightmares." I said hopefully as I dragged myself to bed.

Once there, I tossed and turned, making such a mess of the blankets that both animals jumped off and settled on their own beds. So much for the chamomile tea helping me sleep. Tomorrow afternoon, I'd be meeting the ladies at their version of a coven. The butterflies wouldn't let my stomach settle. In addition to nerves about attending a coven, we had a council meeting in the morning. I didn't trust Roberto and the others not to try something drastic to gain followers. As I finally drifted off, images of monsters with Roberto's face chased me in my dreams.

In the nightmare, my attacker chased me into a corner, a dead end in a corridor with no way out. He started throwing magic balls that hit the walls around me with a *thud. Thud, thud, thud.* As one hit me in the stomach I woke with a jolt. Cinnamon sat on my stomach, gently tapping my cheek with her paw and Sprinkles jumped up and down beside my bed as a large *thud, thud, thud* sounded from somewhere in the cottage.

I leapt out of bed, adrenaline coursing through my body. "Show me what's making the noise," I told my pets. Both ran to the back door. The thumping noise became louder the closer we got. Tentatively I opened the door, wishing I'd thought to pick up a weapon of some sort. In my secure, gated backyard, the wattle tree had split and fallen. Its branches were swinging at a weird angle that caused the *thud, thud*, as it swung against the back of my cottage. It was only as I started to close the door that I saw the word, scrawled in red paint across the trunk. *Beware!*

Though it was a little after 4am, the rising sun illuminated the sky enough for me to take a couple of photos with my mobile. I wanted to clean up the mess, but wisdom said to leave it until Ned or Sophie checked the area. "It's too early to ring the police station now," I told my menagerie. "We're not in any danger," I continued, trying to convince myself. In my experience people who were planning to cause harm, didn't warn their victims first. "An early breakfast for you guys, while I do some research."

Cinnamon walked around my legs, while Sprinkles jumped all over the black leggings I wore as pyjamas. I sorted their food, and Bert's, before boiling the kettle. Armed with a cup of peppermint tea, an apple and my laptop I started an internet search. Social media blogs about Robbie Banks the entrepreneur appeared around the same time that information on Roberto Patri dried up. The man I investigated disappeared without a trace six months before Banks Entertainment and affiliated businesses started popping up. Robbie and the Hartly brothers were board members on shared businesses and other philanthropic organisations.

A search of Misty Vale revealed what I already knew – that our village was a popular destination for grey nomads and those who loved bespoke crafts. The articles I found included tales of the mystical and magical powers some of our inhabitants possessed.

The untidy handwriting on the tree wasn't the first threat I'd received. It went with the job of policewoman and private investigator. I wasn't worried about it. Roberto was an annoying bully but he wasn't dangerous.

I stood and stretched, needing to move my body. After a quick shower I dressed for the day. Through my window I watched the sun as it slowly peeped above the horizon. "Let's go for a walk," I told my excited pup as I clicked the lead onto his collar. "Back soon," I told Bert and Cinnamon as I closed the front door behind me. January in Misty Vale was hot, even this early in the morning. A dry heat. Broken only by the summer rains that started and stopped, like dodgy plumbing. My jeans were comfortable. My white slip-on shoes and my purple shirt sensible, and sun smart. Using the hair tie on my wrist I tied my long brown hair into a high pigtail.

"Good morning, Jane." I recognised Ned's voice as his little blue hatchback pulled up beside me. I felt my mouth morph into a smile at the sound of his voice. Not yet in his uniform, his dimpled smile, dark wavy hair, deep dreamy eyes, made my heart flutter. "Do you have time for a cuppa at The Milky Bar?"

"That sounds fantastic! Sprinkles and I can walk home afterwards," I replied. As Ned popped open the hatch, I lifted Sprinkles into the back of the car. He settled onto the cushion next to a blue plastic crate that held a bunch of sports equipment.

My heart thumped with excitement as I slid in beside the policeman. I enjoyed Ned's company and looked forward to our meals and cuppas together. I was nearly certain he felt the same. My grandmother nodded wisely when I defended my position that a meal with the handsome policeman wasn't a date. "Hazel and I were meeting for breakfast before the council meeting. I'll text her that I'll meet her at the café." I sent a quick message to my grandma on my mobile, before turning my attention to Ned. "Did you manage to get a break last night, or did the weird incidents continue?"

"By midnight all the magical events seemed to peter out. Thankfully it was a quiet crime night. No break ins or thefts reported," Ned replied as he parked his car.

I remembered the incident at my house. "Um, while I think of it, someone broke into my backyard at some point during the night and knocked over a tree. They left a threatening message."

Ned looked concerned. "Are you okay?"

"Yes, we're fine. I'm annoyed and I want to clean it up, but I'd like you or Sophie to dust for prints or at least check it out." I lifted Sprinkles out of the back of the car. Once we arrived at the café, I tied his lead to the metal bike rack outside the café. "We won't be long, then we'll go for that walk," I told him as he waggled his tail excitedly.

Jess beamed as we entered, "Jane, Ned, it's lovely to see you. What can I get for you?" The cafe was already buzzing with customers lined up for coffee, morning muffins, and toasted sandwiches. The two young elves were busy behind the counter. Kat was busy making the customer drinks, while Kit plated up the food.

I surveyed the dainty cakes in the glass cabinet at the front counter. "Is it too early for a cake?" I grinned. "How about a lemon poppyseed muffin and a mocha please." I settled on a slightly bittersweet combo. "When Hazel arrives, I'll pay for whatever she wants to have as well."

"I'll have the same. It sounds like the breakfast of champions," Ned grinned.

I chose a table along the side wall, so I could watch people coming and going. Ned slipped into the booth seat next to me, sending pleasant shivers through my body. "Let's see, do I have this right? You're out walking early in the morning, because you can't sleep, and because of the break in. You're worried about meeting Shaz, Maz, Rosie, and Jazz in their coven, and anxious about the town meeting and how Roberto fits into all of it?" My friend placed his hand gently on top of mine.

Before I could respond, Jess arrived at our table. "Here you are, cuppas in takeaway mugs in case you get called away, a plate of muffins and I'll take Hazel's order when she arrives," she said, placing the goodies on the table in front of us.

"Thanks Jess," we responded in unison. I felt the heat rise in my cheeks as I realised, we were still holding hands.

As Jess returned to the counter, the café door opened, and Hazel walked through. She caught our eye before heading to the counter to place her order. I'd left enough money at the counter for whatever Hazel chose. "Good morning to you both, and you granddaughter of mine, thank you for buying breakfast, but you know you didn't have to." I nodded at Hazel. I'd made enough money as a private eye for the elite that I didn't have to work again for a long time, but still I liked to think I was frugal, or sensible with my money.

I jumped up and hugged my grandma, releasing her so she could join us at the table. "You've done so much for me, the least I can do is shout a coffee from time to time."

"You two look like you were deep in conversation, what did I miss?" she asked.

Ned eyed me over the top of the takeaway mug. I shrugged, not minding if he included Hazel in the discussion.

I smiled back over the top of mine. "We were discussing my lack of sleep and whether the events of the last few days may be contributing factors. I'm probably making too big a deal of it all. My words, not Ned's."

Ned half frowned at me. "I don't think you're overacting. I'd be scared if I was invited to be part of a coven, or even to visit a coven. The council meeting is a big deal too. I don't trust Brad or David. I'd suggest caution. Now please show me the photo you took. I'll take Sprinkles home if you like, when I check the damage."

I handed Ned my phone with the photo of the tree on the screen. "The spare key for the back door is under the rubber mat," I whispered. "I know, it's not a safe hiding place, and I'll think of another one, but if you could pop Sprinkles inside and lock the door, I'll pick up the key later."

"I'll message you when I leave your place." Ned left, his unspoken plea for me to be careful was written all over his face.

Hazel raised an eyebrow. She didn't have to ask, I knew she'd observed the subtle communication between us. I told her about the broken tree and warning message.

"I have some unsettling news also," Hazel began, pausing as Jess handed her a large takeaway mug. "It seems all the other council members have come down with some form of nasty stomach bug. We've had to postpone the meeting until they recover."

"Not a coincidence," I stated the obvious.

"No, not a coincidence," Grandma agreed. "I suggest we spend the morning sorting through the applications, and if possible, interviewing the applicants. We'll report on those meetings when the council convenes." Hazel eyed me as she nibbled on one of the muffins.

"You've already scheduled the meetings," I commented, reading her mind.

She nodded. "When I heard from the council members I contacted each of the applicants and rescheduled their appointments. Brad and his cronies declined their invitations, stating we already know their plans," she added.

I am surprised they weren't eager to visit and tell us about their marvellous ideas," I mused. "How many other applicants are there?" I asked. My stomach gurgled, reminding me I'd left my apple uneaten on the kitchen table. I chose a muffin and savoured the tart citrusy flavours.

"Five. So far. Three locals and two people who are new to the village." Hazel consulted her watch. "I didn't sleep much either. I've put together a plan, and a schedule of the interviews. We'll have time to print copies. The first applicant meeting isn't until 8:30am."

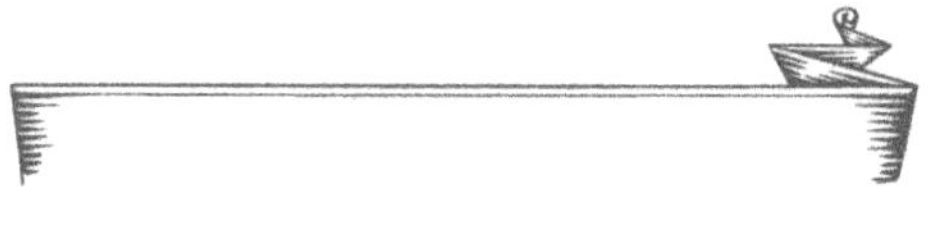

Chapter Eleven

Minerva Elliot wore a long flowing blue kaftan with wide flappy sleeves. I wondered how she got any work done. The loose-fitting clothes would drive me crazy, I'd worry my sleeves would get caught in something, and I'd trip over the hem. "I've always wanted to open an art gallery," she spoke dreamily, as if she were already in her gallery in some other version of her world. She held her head, tilted slightly to one side, her eyes staring into the distance.

Hazel held her pen firmly in her hand. "Do you have a location, or a specific building in mind?"

"I'm leaving those details to the universe to provide. Brad said he could help find the perfect location," she gushed, clapping her hands together quickly, three times. Tiny, shiny, silver stars fluttered from her fingertips out into the room before fading to nothingness. Minerva clasped her hands together, her fingers wiggling ever slow slightly. I felt a breeze tickle the back of my neck.

"I see," Hazel replied as she made notes.

I jotted down some words too, describing her aura. Her thoughts were harder to read, every word I caught, disappeared like the stars. Were air elementals all so, flighty? "How many artists are on your books, ready to showcase their works? Are they local, or from further afield?"

Minerva stared at me like I was bonkers. *Pot calling kettle* I thought, as I read her mind. "There's no need for me to worry about those details. They'll find me when the time is right. I leave that sort of thing to the universe. The wind will bring me what I need."

Hazel got to her feet. "Thank you for coming to talk to us today," she tried to shake Minerva's hand, but our guest tucked her hands into her sleeves. The artist wandered out the door without any further prompting from us. The outer door shut with a whoosh as the air elemental left the building.

"Absolutely bonkers," I stated as my bottom landed back on my chair.

"Loopy as a loon," Hazel agreed.

"Who's next?" I consulted my notes.

I didn't have to wait long to find out. Hazel had barely finished telling me about Tricia Riley, a local earth elemental, who owned the local nursery and had plans to extend, when there was a knock at the door.

On the other side of the door stood a smiling lady carrying two pots of bright pink and yellow flowers. I estimated Tricia was a few years older than me. Her long brown hair was neatly plaited to the back. She wore a floppy garden hat, tan jeans and an oversized crème shirt. "You must be Tricia, I'm Jane, come in, we've set up in our office." I led our interviewee into our shared space.

Tricia placed the pots in the table. "Hazel, it's lovely to see you." she shook my grandma's hand. "Jane, it's lovely to finally meet you properly. I know you've been into the nursery, but we'd not formally met. Please accept these dahlias as gifts, I thought they were so pretty, I wanted to share, and I'm excited to share my ideas with you." She reached into her handbag and pulled out a manilla folder.

"Please have a seat. Would you like a cup of tea, coffee, or a glass of water?" Hazel motioned to the spare seat at the side of the table.

Tricia shook her head. "Thank you but I finished a cup of dandelion tea not long ago." She handed us both groups of pages kept together by paperclips, keeping the third bundle for herself. "Here's a summary of my proposal, with the detail behind it. In addition to my nursery, I have a farm on the edge of town. It's been a dream to establish a business where I grow and sell plants from seeds. All grown here, on my farm, sourcing seeds from the local area, and bespoke, difficult to locate olde-worldy plants. I've got quotes for all the equipment and set up, and ongoing costs. I'd like to extend the nursery into the empty building next to it. I've included my trading figures for the last few years as well." She folded her hands neatly on top of her notes. Her aura was serene but with a hint of nervous energy. Tricia wanted this opportunity.

"I'm impressed, I can see how much time and effort you've put into this," Hazel said admiringly. "Is this something you've been thinking about for a while?"

"Oh gosh yes," she replied. "This has been a dream of mine for so long. I hesitated to apply, because I don't know what I think of Brad Hartly." Tricia stopped speaking, worried she'd over stepped.

I smiled to put her at ease. "Please don't worry. Anything said in here stays between us."

"We're evaluating each proposal on their own merits, not in conjunction with any other application. I haven't spoken with Jane in detail yet, but we may have grants available, depending on what the business can offer the village. I'd be grateful if you didn't tell anyone I said that," Hazel spoke softly. If she shared that information with Tricia, she must've been impressed by her project plans. "We'll be sharing your application and our recommendation with the council later in the week."

As Tricia left, after a conversation that included the best plants to grow from seed in the summer, a man walked through the door to our office, without knocking.

"Troy Ryan." The man's voice was terse. He was young, I estimated in his late twenties. His firm handshake, and the confidence oozing from every pore of his body – could he be related to Brad Hartly?

"Good morning, it's nice to meet you Troy, I'm Hazel and this is Jane. Please sit." She motioned to the spare chair as we took ours.

His aura bristled as she spoke. He didn't like being told what to do.

Hazel consulted her notes. "Your application is to develop an events planning business that will also provide training in event planning and hospitality. Can you tell us a little about what drew you to Misty Vale as the place to establish your business?"

Troy squared his shoulders, adjusting his navy jacket on his tall but slightly built frame. "I certainly can! With the unique gifts of the locals, the bespoke businesses already established in the town, and the upcoming entertainment centre, it's a perfect fit."

I raised an eyebrow. A hospitality and event training venue would be one of the last businesses I would expect to find in Misty Vale. Troy was quoting his application word for word. I flipped through the applications. Brad's, David's and Robbie's paperwork contained the exact same words. "Have you worked with the Hartly brothers and Robbie Banks before?"

My question caught him off guard. Troy stared at me. He looked at Hazel, and she returned his gaze. "The business world is all about making connections." He said averting his eyes as he pulled his phone out of his pocket. After pressing a couple of buttons, he held it to his ear. "Okay, yes I see, I'll be right there." He jumped out of his seat, sending an apologetic look at Hazel. "An emergency, I must go. Thanks, let me know when I can start building." Before either of us could utter a word, he left the office, the outer door shutting behind him.

"We'll be recommending not to progress that particular application," Hazel said as she made notes on the paper in front of her. "Were we meant to believe he received a call? The worst acting I've seen for a while."

"I agree. It's a no from us to Mr Troy Ryan from the city," I added.

"Candy Sweets is next," Grandma read from her list. "She lives out of town, and sells handmade sweets, lollies and chocolates at the local markets. In her application she requests to be able to park her gypsy van in the main street and sell her wares from it, six days a week."

"I look forward to her presentation," I commented. As we waited, I scribbled notes to remind me of the previous applicants.

The pianola text tone of Hazel's mobile broke the silence. "We won't be talking to Candy today," I heard the disappointment in her voice. "There's a large tree down on the road into the village and the removal crew sent her back home."

"Oh no, I hope she'll reschedule once the road is clear." I consulted my list. "We only have one more applicant, Casey Sparks. Is she related to Marigold Sparks?"

"He's her grandson, a strong fire elemental, recently home after studying overseas." Hazel moved to her desk, where she had arranged seven folders. "He's keen to set up a place for people of all ages to learn crafting skills. Working with clay to make pottery. Teaching woodwork skills to empower people to build their own furniture. Metal sculpture work is mentioned as well." She re-read his application. "There's a vacant building a block back from the main street which he has suggested would be suitable for his project."

While we waited, I made us coffees in the kitchenette adjacent to our office. Wishing we had biscuits or berries and nuts to eat, I made a mental note to pick up supplies next time I went to the supermarket.

Casey was seated at the table when I returned. "Would you like something to drink – water, tea or coffee?" I asked after Grandma introduced us.

Casey stood to shake my hand. "No thank you. I was telling Hazel how excited I am to be home after three years overseas. When I think about Misty Vale, I think about honouring those who have served us over the years. People in caring and support roles, nurses, teachers, and military. Those who never ask for help for themselves."

"Why did you identify that particular building?" I asked, watching him over the top of my cup. I inhaled the warmth and bitter aroma of my brew.

"My grandfather worked there, building wooden furniture. He was a real craftsman, and a gentleman. I'd love to be able to honour him." He handed Hazel a thumb drive. "I've taken pictures of the items I'm planning to make. There's an outline of the workshop I propose to teach." He looked at me apologetically. "I only made one copy."

"That's fine, we can share the information," I reassured him.

I sipped my coffee while Casey and Hazel reminisced about Misty Vale and its residents. The clock told me I had little under an hour before the coven meeting. I gulped away my trepidation.

"Let's make notes of today's interviews, so we can brief the council members when we meet." Grandma suggested, as she collected my empty coffee mug.

"We still have to meet Brad, David, Robbie, and Candy," I reminded her.

She side-eyed me. "Yes, although those three men declined my initial invitation to meet. I would like to know more about their proposals. I've a feeling we'll be receiving more applicants before the day is over." She lined up her notebook and the printed applications on the left side of her computer. "We can discuss the applications later. You have a meeting to prepare for. Just remember, they are four women, like you, or me. There's nothing scary about them," Hazel's words broke through my thoughts.

"That's true," I replied.

"Magic, spell work, and covens, are as old and natural as the trees in the local bushland. It's about the old ways of doing things. Don't be concerned about not knowing what to do. It's about instinct, intuition, intention. The others will guide you," Hazel added.

I knew she was only trying to help. Nevertheless, my anxiety had a mind of its own. My stomach cramped and twisted, even when I attempted to apply logic. I shook my head to clear my thoughts and focused on the task at hand. Making sense of the notes I made during the interviews.

My heart thumped wildly, as I counted the five wooden steps that led to a small porch. Ivy geranium, jasmine, and wisteria covered the wooden beams framing the entry into Maz's cottage. I exhaled, releasing my anxiety. Before I could knock at the door, it opened. My friend's smiling face greeted me.

Maz's dark hair, peppered with grey, was wound into a bun at the back of her head. She wore a calico apron over a summery green dress. "Do come in Jane. The others are already here. If it's okay with you, we'll get started. We'll have tea and coffee afterwards." She eyed me, worriedly. I wondered if she could hear my erratic heartbeat. "There's nothing to be scared about. We are merely a group of friends messing around with the elements, having fun."

If she thought her words would make me feel better, they didn't. I handed her the plastic container with caramel slice. "For afterwards," my voice squeaked.

Maz smiled warmly, as she took the container and linked her arm through mine. She whispered something about looking forward to the afternoon.

I couldn't help feeling I was being taken somewhere scary. *Nonsense,* I told myself. *Everything will be okay. This is your heritage.* And besides, Hazel wouldn't have suggested I meet this group of women if she thought I'd be in any harm.

"Hello Jane, welcome," Jazz, Rosie, and Shaz chorused as Maz led me into a large, glass walled living room. Beyond the glass was a garden filled with plants. I recognised only a few of the flowering plants I could spy beyond Shaz and Jazz's heads. I turned my focus to the four women in the room as I sat in the chair Maz offered, between Rosie and herself.

The table and chairs were made of old sturdy wood. In the middle of the table a black cauldron sat on top of a bright red placemat made of thicky woven material. The cast iron pot stood about twenty centimetres tall if you included its legs. The room smelt of clove, citrus, aniseed, rosemary, and cinnamon.

"We cheat a little. The simmer pot is a big saucepan with oranges, cloves, cinnamon and other herbs bubbling and simmering on the stove. The cauldron has an unique heat source. We only use it on special occasions." Had Maz read my mind? It was racing, so she would've done well to do so.

"The cards on the table are our focus for the day, the items in front of us are our tools," Jazz's voice held a solemn tone. A set of tarot cards lay spread out on the table around the cauldron. Red woven mats, smaller versions of the mat under the cauldron, sat as placemats in front of us. Jazz's blonde curly hair gave an air of fairy magic, or maybe elvin magic. At least that's the image that popped into my head as I listened to her quiet singsong voice. Her pale skin and green eyes enhanced the magic aura around the table.

Shaz leant towards me as she continued my first instruction into the workings of a coven. "Crystals are one of the tools we use with our elemental magic, to create, focus, set intentions and boost our powers." Her flaming red hair was tied back into a ponytail. Little butterfly clips sat nestled in her hair. Her long red nails pointed at each rock as she spoke. "Maz's rock is emerald. For grounding, balance and healing. Rosie uses moonstone for wisdom, healing and protection. Jazz's stone is clear quartz. Intuition, clarity, manifestation. Mine, tiger's eye, is for perseverance and focus. We chose amethyst for you. It will bring you peace, strengthen your intuition, and spiritual growth, while enhancing your mental clarity and emotional balance."

"It's the perfect crystal to start with," Rosie added. "We all own one, we were given on our fifteenth birthdays."

I couldn't help smiling. At fifteen I was full of teenage angst, planning to leave home, never to return. "Great, you do realise I'm a lot older than that," I joked. "I've got a lot of catching up to do." I picked up the little purple crystal. About the size of a medium strawberry, it fitted nicely in the palm of my hand. "Is it normal that the stone feels warm against my skin?" I asked in wonder as the sunlight entering from the large windows caught the colours of the little sharp angles.

"Yes," Shaz replied with a smile. "It's an indication the crystal is meant for you." She saw my puzzled look and continued. "There's a lot of myth around whether we should choose our own magic items, or whether they should be gifts from others. I like to think it's a little of both. If something is meant to be yours, you'll know it, instinctively."

"That makes sense." I turned the crystal over in my palm, before placing it in front of me. "My grandmother has a shelf full of crystals, rocks, cards, books and other items. I haven't asked her about them, yet. I think she wants to make sure I don't run away, when she tells me more about the family I didn't know I belonged to."

I felt four pairs of eyes staring at me.

"Hazel has taught me so much already and answered all my questions." I looked around at my new friends. "The problem is, I don't know what I don't know, or what to ask. She is taking it slowly, guiding and showing me how to make sense of my powers." I didn't add out loud that a part of me was scared to hear the whole truth. Running away wasn't an option anymore. Misty Vale and my cottage were my home, my safety net. I didn't want anything to jeopardise that.

"The amethyst will help you learn more about who you are. It'll strengthen your intuition, your powers and your confidence." Rosie offered, leaving me wondering whether the women around the table could read my mind.

I decided to change the subject. "What are the other items on the table?"

Rosie picked up the notepad closest to her. "We each have a notepad and pens, for jotting down ideas, spells, things that come to us when we are gathered." The notebooks were thick, with material covers. Jazz's was a cream colour, Rosie's a dark blue, Shaz's notebook was red, and Maz held a green book. The book in front of me was covered in a dark purple material. My hand hovered over it, tingling as my fingers reached for the item. The pens reminded me of artists watercolours. Each writing implement were similar in colour to their corresponding books.

Shaz waved her hand in front of her, lighting the five white pillar candles. I blinked. "Candles are one of my favourite tools," she grinned. "I don't need a lighter or matches. It comes in handy."

"Does that ring you are wearing have something to do with your powers?" I pointed at the gold ring with the small red stone on her right hand.

"Indirectly. It was my grandmother's. Through it I channel her powers and connect with her." Shaz held her hand out for me to examine the ring more closely.

"We all have jewellery that connects us to our powers." Maz fiddled with the silver bracelet on her wrist. "I found this at a second-hand shop. I'd been dreaming about a bracelet like this one, for months. A clear case of a magic tool finding its rightful owner."

Rosie touched a silver dolphin on the chain around her neck. "My best friend in primary school gave me this trinket. It mightn't be true silver, but it's linked to my magic in a way I don't question."

Jazz held her hands out, palm side up. "My ring is on a necklace that I leave at home. My magic works more effectively when I don't wear jewellery."

My hand moved to my neck, playing with an imaginary pendant. When I closed my eyes, I saw the pendant clearly. A grey metal chain, with two small stones, one red and the other purple. A ruby and amethyst.

I held out my right hand, where my multicoloured ring sat, it's stones glistening in the sunlight. "I found this in a box I've carried around for years. Did it appear when I needed it? Did my parents or an ancestor put it there? All I know is my powers seem to have grown since I put it on. During the week of the crazy Christmas parade."

"It's so pretty," Shaz whispered, "With stones for each element and each emotion."

"The different stones glow stronger, depending on what's going on around me, and how I feel," I conceded.

Maz touched her neck, "You touched your neck before. You sense your necklace, another talisman, don't you?" Maz spoke quietly. "You'll find it soon." She touched her neck again. "I have a necklace that belongs with my bracelet, but I lost it. It's finding its way back to me.

I had no answer to that.

Maz's voice took on a lyrical quality. "Now, we close our eyes and pick a card. Not with our hands, but with our minds." I wanted to peek, but I kept my eyes tightly shut. I heard what sounded like a rustling of the cards, not shuffling exactly. I concentrated on the cards.

"Concentrate," a voice whispered. I couldn't place the voice. Concentrate on what? The voice? The cards? I tried to remember what I knew about tarot. The point was to find answers to questions, solve mysteries, find true love etc. What did I want to know the answer to? My magic. I wanted to know what my magic was all about and how to tune into it more. I felt a whoosh of air as a card landed on the table in front of me.

"That's the last one; we can open our eyes now," Maz voice broke through my thoughts.

I slowly opened my eyes. Five tarot cards lay, face down on the table in front of us. My mind wandered as Maz and the others talked about the cards they found in front of them. I caught the gist of the words, *moving forward, new projects, counting blessings, paying attention, resting when needed...*

It felt a little like I was eavesdropping. Plus, it appeared I had my own whispering voice in my head...*you can do this, you are magic, it is part of you, believe, trust.* I blinked, trying to dislodge the ghostly voice stuck in a loop in my head. I realised the others were staring at me.

"Are you okay?" Shaz's hand hovered, like she wanted to touch mine, but wasn't sure if she should.

My cheeks warmed, as I slowly shook my head. "I'm okay, I mean, I think I am. Am I the only one who can hear voices?"

The others nodded knowingly.

"The cards are talking to you," Maz explained. "Our first time, when we were teens, the voices followed us for weeks. We each have our own decks. If you don't have your own set, The Magic Cauldron, in town is a good place to start."

I wanted to pinch myself. Had I woken up in some fairy tale, or more accurately, a magical witch tale? "Did it take long, for you to get used to the voices, the intuition, the mind reading?"

"Oh gosh, that was so long ago, and we were all going through it at the same time." Jazz looked at the others and shrugged. "For us, it was part of growing up. A rite of passage."

Rosie pointed to my card, "Would you like to talk about your card?"

I nodded as I turned the card over to reveal The High Priestess.

"Nice," Jazz explained the card, "This card is linked to intuition, wisdom, and inner knowledge. Reminding you that you have the ability to gain insights into your own magical skills and helping you to connect with a deeper understanding of your own power."

Maz pulled her chair out and stood. "I think we need a cuppa and some sugary treats. I fear we're overwhelming our new friend, and we don't want to make her too scared to come back." She smiled at me.

Shaz pushed her chair back too. "Jane, why don't you come with me. The table on the verandah is set up for tea." I let Shaz lead me through the glass sliding door to the modular grey metal table and chair setting. Five matching chairs, not four and a makeshift one because I was an unexpected visitor.

Jazz and Rosie joined us as we sat, with my container of slice, a tray of ham and cheese sandwiches, strawberries, and grapes. Maz slid a tray with five mugs of coffee in the middle rectangular glass topped table.

An hour later I sat at my kitchen bench, mulling over the day's events. My budgie tweeted his thanks to the pile of seed I poured into his bowl. Cinnamon rubbed her side against my legs as a thank you for her food. After scoffing his food, Sprinkles tried to jump on my lap, to see what I held in my hands. "Maz let me bring these things home, as long as I returned them next week. When the coven meets again," I showed him each item. The small piece of amethyst, the purple notebook and pen, and the high priestess card. "I wonder if Hazel would come with me to the magic shop. I don't know how I feel about going there by myself." Sprinkles licked my hand. My conversation with my pets was interrupted by the beeping of my mobile.

I recognised my grandmothers voice straight away. "Do you want to meet for a coffee early tomorrow morning? If we meet at The Milky Bar we can do a spot of shopping at the magic shop afterwards."

"That sounds perfect," I responded, looking forward to catching up with my only living relative. "The coven was interesting, but not what I expected. I think it made me more curious about my gifts." I didn't ask how she knew I wanted to go to the magic shop. I was slowly getting used to being able to communicate on a level that didn't require words.

Hazel broke into my thoughts. "I've got a couple items I want you to have. I'll bring them tomorrow." A few minutes later, after promising to try for a good night's sleep, I put down my phone.

I yawned, as I clicked the switch on the kettle. "Do I curl up and read a book, or clean up that mess outside?" I asked Bert, remembering the early morning's excitement. I opened the back door, expecting to be faced with the task of removing the dead tree. All trace of the mess had disappeared. Where the tree grew twenty-four hours earlier a small potted tree stood in its place. The tag on the tree said, *I hope you like your new tree. I've got paperwork to catch up on this evening, let's meet for breakfast tomorrow. Ned x.*

Chapter Twelve

Voices whispering my name had me tossing and turning for most of the night. "Just once I'd love to be able to say I'd had a good night sleep," I told my pets as I followed them to the kitchen. While my family ate, I contemplated the contents of my pantry. Opting for peppermint tea, I closed my eyes and inhaled the aroma. Thoughts hovered out of reach at the edge of my brain. I concentrated on the thin threads of silver as they danced in front of my eyes. *Excitement, enchantment, watch out...*

The words make no sense," I told Bert. He chirped sympathetically in response. "Maybe it's *excitement* at seeing Ned and Hazel, and *enchantment* because I want to go to the magic shop. The warning to *watch out* could be referring to several things." I gulped down the anxiety I felt rising in my body.

Jeans were comfortable. Easy to run in, if I needed to escape a situation. Not that I felt the need to run, in Misty Vale. Comfortable flat black shoes, and a pink shirt. My long hair tied in a ponytail high on the top of my head. Since Hazel stepped up as mayor, and I became her assistant, I took a little more care with what I wore each day.

"Now you be good," I told my furry family. It would be so easy to stay home, work in my garden or start a new craft project. My emotions were a little raw after seeing Roberto, experiencing my first coven meeting, and interviewing the applicants the previous day. "That would be breaking the promise I made to myself," I told myself in the mirror. "I'm not changing my routine because I'm a little jumpy."

I inhaled, held my breath, exhaling slowly. The trepidation building in my stomach eased. I wiggled my fingers, releasing some pent-up energy. I closed my eyes for a second. Sprinkles jumped up, his paws reaching my knees. I opened my eyes and smiled at my furry companion. "I'm meeting with Ned and Hazel. I'll probably be home after lunch," I told my pets. Bert chirped happily, Sprinkles ran around in circles and Cinnamon sat curled up on her cushion, with one eye on me.

Slowly she uncurled herself and headed over to me. Instinctively I crouched, with the tools Maz leant me. Cinnamon sniffed each one. She swotted each of them out of my hand. "Is it the items you have a problem with, or the person?" I tried to ignore my fear as I watched my feline for clues. My stomach flip flopped at the thought that I couldn't trust my new friends. "Okay Cinnamon, help me not overthink this. Grandma suggested I befriend the group. I'll get my own tools and return theirs." My feline walked up to me, nudging my chin. "Okay, thanks." I patted my familiar. After tucking the items into a paper gift bag that I placed on the table near my door, I glanced at the time on my kitchen clock, said goodbye to my pets and locked the door behind me.

My energy felt lighter than usual as I walked the few hundred metres to the main street. I waved at my next-door neighbour Margo, and Mr Quinn, an elderly man who was often out pottering in his garden as I passed by. Cathy opened the door to The Crafty Owl, as I walked past. "It's so hot these days, I decided to open early. Many of our crafters are early risers," she smiled.

"That's a great idea. I'll probably be back in later, with Hazel," I smiled at my fellow craft enthusiast.

As I approached the café Ned messaged to say he'd been caught up at an incident, and he'd try and catch up later. My heart sank in disappointment that I wouldn't be seeing Ned for breakfast.

I saw Hazel as soon as I opened the door. She was already seated at our table, the booth against the far wall, from where we could see all who came and left the café, but couldn't be seen by anyone, unless they were looking for us. On the table sat two mugs, one with white tea for my grandmother and a mocha for me, and a plate of plate of fruit filled muffins.

"How did you know Ned wasn't going to be able to make breakfast? Or didn't I let you know he was going to join us?" I asked as I hugged Grandma.

"I may have the equivalent of a police radio. It may have told me Ned and Sophie are busy investigating a series of incidents," she replied.

Maybe, one day, my intuition would be as strong as Hazel's. If I stopped doubting myself.

Less than half an hour later, I'd filled Hazel in on the details of the meeting at Maz's. including Cinnamon's reaction to the items. As I finished speaking, Jess arrived at the table. "Can I get you anything else? Another cuppa, or more muffins."

My grandmother smiled, "Thank you Jess, but not at the moment. Jane and I have an important appointment. We may return later."

To get to The Magic Cauldron we crossed the road at the end of the main street. Seeing the old school yard brought back memories of the chaotic Christmas parade a month ago, when a bunch of animated creatures fought each other, and a group of elves. "I'm glad you were here, to help me get that situation under control." Hazel gently steered me away from the memories of the mayhem.

Down a short cobblestone alleyway sat a small row of shops. "Why have I never noticed this street before?" I asked. My eyes widened, taking in the ambience, the black brick walls, the worn grey paver stones under my feet, and the golden script above the shop windows.

"Because you weren't looking for it," was her simple reply.

The Magic Cauldron was the third in a row of three shops. "Relax, the shops aren't as scary as they look," my grandmother said as we passed Rustic Rocks and Mystic Shadows. I touched the cold black brick façade that ran the length of the row of shops. How had I missed seeing these? Even if I wasn't looking, these establishments stood out.

"I bet there's a lot to Misty Vale you've not noticed yet. I suspect that will change as you grow into your powers."

Before I could ask her what she meant exactly, she opened the door to The Magic Cauldron. A tall skinny woman, her face covered in lines that came with age, and a shock of iridescent purple hair met us as we crossed the threshold. "Ah Hazel, you came. This must be Clara. You look so much like your mother," she addressed me. My spine tingled, and a couple of sparks flew from my fingertips before I could stop them. "Oh, don't worry about that, it'll get absorbed in the air." She waved her hand as a ball of coloured light appeared, sweeping up the stray electricity into its middle.

"You have my granddaughter at a disadvantage. She is more comfortable with the name Jane, not Clara. Jane, this is Beatrix, or Trixie to her oldest school friends." The two women embraced, leaving me to take in the odd sights in the shop. Inside was as black as the outside bricks. An effect achieved mostly with velvet and shiny paint from what I could make out in the dimly lit store. The shelves were lined with all manner of items – jars, packs of cards, crystals, books, ingredients for spells, cauldrons, candles, and other items I couldn't name for they were new to me. Tiny lights hovering above us lit the space. I watched fascinated, as the lights slowly changed positions. Were they living beings of light?

Before I could ask, Hazel waved in the direction of the shelf with the books. "Would you like to choose a couple of books and a pack of tarot cards," she said in a voice that made it clear she wasn't merely suggesting I check out the items. I wandered towards the shelves as she followed her friend through a red glittery curtain. Another tingle ran the length of my spine. This time I was ready and held my fingers still, so the sparks stayed where they belonged.

In front of me sat boxes of tarot cards. I squinted at the intricate illustrations. My hand hovered above the packs of cards. One of the smaller boxes, a deep green with warm reds, golds and deep purple, moved from its place, closer to my finger. I should have been surprised, but somehow, in this space, anything was possible. The shelf above the cards held books on a variety of topics – spirit animals, tarot, crystals, spells, potions, and more. Illustrations and embossed titles shimmered, even in the dull lighting. I sensed the intent of each author. Mind reading, intentions, incantations, and other words I didn't understand spun in front of me. I closed my eyes, gulping in some air. When I opened them, two books sat out of place on the shelf. *Simple Witchcraft,* and *Basic Potions and Spells.* As good a starting place as any I could have chosen.

Hazel and Beatrix emerged from behind the shimmery curtain. "I see you've made a selection." Beatrix held out her hand. I placed the two books and the tarot cards on her palm.

My grandmother handed me a small red velvet pouch. "Last night I told you I had a couple of items to give to you. I asked Trixie to check their magic. Many objects act as sponges, collecting remnants of magic from their owners. These items have been in your family for generations. One from your mother's side, and one from your father's, from mine."

My fingers trembled as I tugged the drawstring open. I tipped the contents gently onto my open palm. A thin golden chain necklace lay glistening against my skin. Attached to the chain were two stones, an amethyst in the shape of a teardrop and a smoky quartz piece in the shape of a heart. As with the amethyst at Maz's the crystals felt warm on my skin.

Hazel picked up the necklace, "May I?" I nodded as she opened the clasp and placed the chain around my neck. The little stones sat just below that little part of my throat that tucked in, but not long enough that it disappeared into what little cleavage I possessed. *Wrapped around me like a hug from my family.* As with the ring, the necklace settled in, like it belonged with me, and had been there all my life.

"I pictured this necklace, in detail, the only difference was there was a red stone, not the smoky grey one," I whispered as my fingers touched both crystals. They pulsated with a vibration of their own.

My grandmother gave me a funny look. "When your great grandfather made it, there was a red stone, but it disappeared over one hundred years ago." Hazel's phone beeped once, twice, three times. She sighed, "I suppose that's our cue to go into the office." She turned back to her friend. "Thank you, Trixie, please send me an invoice and I'll transfer the money for the task you did for me, and for the items Jane chose."

I added my thanks as Trixie handed me my books and cards and closed the door behind us.

"Wait, Grandma, you said two items," I said as I felt something else in the little pouch. Juggling the cards and books I pulled an ornate grey metal brooch from the pouch. Smaller than my little finger the piece of jewellery featured one single rose.

"From my side of the family. Wear this brooch only when you need to hide in plain sight. Its magic is strong," Hazel said. Before she could continue her mobile beeped three more times. "Emails and texts from Brad, David and Robbie, asking to meet to discuss their plans. They must think that the more they annoy us with requests, the quicker we will cave in and meet them."

I gave her a wry smile, "Then they don't know us at all."

Chapter Thirteen

"What's this?" I bent to pick up a large white envelope in the middle of the office floor. I tore open the envelope. Inside was a single sheet of paper. "It's a list of the local properties purchased by Brad, David, and Robbie in the last six months, properties the Hartly's already owned, and a list of properties they wanted, but the owners refused to sell." I turned the page. "There's no identification or indication of the sender."

Hazel scanned the paper I handed to her. "Useful," she murmured.

With access to the same inbox, we planned to divide the work between us. "Robbie Banks is a problem," Hazel stated the obvious a few minutes after we started reading through the emails.

I snorted derisively. "He was equally annoying in his previous persona as Roberto Patri."

"My guess is that Brad and David told him about the magic in the village. They're not the first group who've tried to take advantage of us. Greed is a great motivator." Hazel glared at her computer screen. "So much for a quiet start to the day. We should schedule the meetings with Brad and his cronies. Otherwise, they'll be badgering us all day."

"They should have accepted your initial offer to meet. I wonder what they're up to, changing their minds like that. I guess the sooner we meet them, and reject their applications, the sooner things can go back to normal." I scrolled through my emails. "Our inbox is fuller than I expected," I commented, looking up from my screen. "We've got questions about business applications, whether magic can be used openly, what we're doing about the strange happenings."

"I'd forgotten how many enquiries come with this role," Hazel frowned. "Residents asking about the rules of using magic, tourists wanting to know whether magic is real, or if they have to possess magic to live here. Others want to move here and take advantage of the magic and make a fortune. Some locals think they know best and love trying to tell the council what to do, but on the whole, Misty Vale is quiet, peaceful." She waved her arms in the air. "This kerfuffle the Hartly's have conjured, is all aimed to distract us." The documents I'd piled on my desk, ready for filing, flew into the air and sorted themselves into folders.

A gentle knocking at the door interrupted our conversation. "Um, sorry to interrupt, but I thought you'd want to know, it's snowing in the village." Ned's handsome smile melted my heart. I shook myself mentally. *Get a grip Jane, there'll be time for romance later, hopefully.*

My grandmother and I rose from our chairs. "You say village, is it the whole town or specific areas that are being snowed upon?" Hazel reached for her bag.

Ned held the door open as we joined him in the short corridor. "The main shopping area, the school, and the park. The snow front appears to be moving across the village. Sophie is coordinating calls, so far there's been no accidents, but I don't want to jinx us."

"Has this happened before?" I asked my grandmother.

"There are often strange weather patterns. Residents experimenting with their powers, or bouts of anxiety, like the freak storms you cause. The incidents are normally short, sharp, and quickly over," Hazel replied.

"That's my experience, during the years I've lived here," Ned agreed. "If you're happy with the sit, watch, and wait approach," he suggested.

"Hopefully it will blow over," Hazel mused.

"Can we go and see it?" I'd not seen snow since I'd returned from the UK. After ten years there, I missed the white Christmases, though the warmer weather was a nice change.

Ned opened the door. "I hope you have your winter woollies with you," he quipped.

"Who would've thought we'd need a coat in Misty Vale in January?" I marvelled as a blast of cold air hit us as soon as we walked outside.

"I've got a spare coat at the station," Ned offered, noting my lightweight shirt. The policeman wore a light blue collared shirt.

Before I could comment that Ned must be feeling cold as well Hazel offered us both black, long sleeved hooded jackets. She donned a third, smiling in amusement at the looks on our faces. "I may be old, but what's the use of having powers if I can't conjure up a couple of coats when needed."

"Thanks Hazel," Ned and I said together, as we walked further into the fluffy, wet, snow gently falling around us. A light covering had settled on the ground.

"Should we stop the snow, or wait and see how long it lasts?" I wondered aloud.

"As long as there aren't any accidents or complaint calls, we could let it go." Ned responded. "Sophie is sending a drone up to assess the whole area, to see how far the snow is spreading. Although with this low cloud, she'll probably have limited visibility. If it gets worse, or dangerous, could you stop it?"

I nodded. "I think so."

Hazel pulled her mobile out of the pocket of her hoodie. It was slightly bigger than a normal sized phone, I'd been meaning to ask her about that. She ducked under the awning of the dress shop a few doors down from the café. "Let's see," she muttered as she tapped on the keyboard of her electronic device.

"That's not a normal mobile phone, is it?" I asked as the device grew to the size of a tablet.

My grandmother gave me a funny look. "Observant child, I wondered when you'd ask about it. Think of it as google maps specifically for our village." She turned the tablet around so we could see. The snow was limited to a three-block radius around the main street. Which meant my backyard was covered in snow, but hers wasn't. "See this legend here?" She pointed to a row of colours at the top of the screen. Ned and I nodded. "That means the freak weather is created by a person's magic powers. I can't tell if it is deliberate or accidental. But it should ease by early afternoon."

Ned shook his head in wonder. "That's an awfully useful tool Hazel. I don't suppose I can order one for the station."

Hazel tucked the tablet back into her pocket. The device shrunk until it was little bigger than a normal sized phone. "Maybe not, but I may be able to get a version of it for you. Would a laptop based in the station be of any use?"

"It sure would," Ned's eyes lit up. "It'd save us some time and angst if we knew whether an event was magical or not."

I could think of several other useful applications, and additions. I made a note to ask Hazel about the possibilities.

The door to the café opened and a group of people wandered out into the snow. The aroma of Jess's signature coffee blend wafted over to where we were standing. "Does anyone else feel like a coffee, or maybe a hot chocolate?" I asked.

"Let me message Sophie, and I'll join you for a few minutes," Ned replied.

My grandmother snuck me a glance as we walked through the café door. She approved of the slowly blossoming relationship between the handsome policeman and me.

I screwed up my face as a loud voice rang out through the café. "This little village is the perfect setting for one of our magical makeovers. A tourist destination innocently waiting to be discovered. We'll have people visiting by the thousands. Once we build it, they will come."

My fingers balled up into tight fists. Hazel tapped my hand gently, reminding me to unclench my fist before I started a freak thunderstorm, or worse. The weather was wacky enough already. I let my fingers hang loosely as she led me to a table near the entrance. From my position I couldn't see the table where Roberto, or Robbie as he called himself, was entertaining a group of businessmen. "Stay here, count to fifty, think about Ned, I'll get us some drinks," she whispered. I nodded, already counting, and concentrating on my breathing.

Ned and my grandmother returned at the same time. "I heard you mention Robbie Banks when I called into the office earlier," the policeman spoke quietly as he slid into the booth next to me. "I meant to tell you that Sophie's conducted further investigations into Robbie, and his alter ego Roberto. Both personas had business dealings with the Hartlys. They are connected to several major corporations here and overseas. Their names are associated with various shady dealings. There's not enough evidence to send them to gaol, yet."

I nodded. "As Roberto Patri, he was obnoxious, less than honest, a bully of a man. He stole millions of dollars from several companies and was involved in thefts of rare art. I proved it, but he escaped and evaded the authorities. That was five years ago." I focused on the variety of delicious looking cakes in the glass cabinet at the front counter. "I can't quite believe it is a coincidence that we both end up in Misty Vale, but I don't think he'd bother following me. Now I know he already knew the Hartlys that explains his arrival in our village."

Ned turned to Hazel. "Do you know if Misty Vale is well known as a place with magic? Is there a register of towns where magic is used, or does that sound totally crazy?"

My grandmother frowned. "I've been out of the loop, a virtual hermit for thirty years. It'd be reasonable to expect that a lot has changed in that time, so yes, it's possible. Florence and her cronies were hoping to attract tourists. The Hartlys will be encouraging visitors and tourists to spend their money here."

Before we could comment further Jess arrived with four large take-away mugs. "Here you go, this should keep you warm and cozy. I don't mind the change of weather, as long as it's back to normal soon."

I smiled at our friend. "Yes, I'm sure the sun will be out again in no time."

Ned chose the mugs with his and Sophie's name on them. "If you don't mind, I'll head back to the station. Get this to Sophie while it's hot." He turned to Hazel, "Let me know how much the computer will cost, and I'll apply for a grant."

"Why don't you call into Jane's after work? You can update each other, and Jane can fill me in later," my grandmother added, a mischievous grin on her face.

Ned's cheeks reddened. I felt the flush on mine too. "I finish around five," his voice croaked a little as he got the words out.

I knew exactly how he felt. "I'll have something light ready for dinner," my voice sounded similarly odd. I felt like a teenager going on a date.

"Fabulous," Hazel replied for us both. "Come on Jane, we'll take our cuppas back to the office, we've got some work to do."

Chapter Fourteen

A large parcel, wrapped in brown paper sat outside the door to the inner office. The building we occupied as the council office used to be the local switchboard, back when there were three-digit telephone numbers. Women, mostly, sat in a room with lights and cables in front of them, connecting locals to each other, and occasionally listening in. Or so Hazel told me. I was born of a generation where push buttons replaced the old dial telephones. The building also housed the local community services and administration for local contractors. The outer door was unlocked at 7am and not locked again until 9pm. Anyone could have walked in and left the parcel for Hazel.

"Should we get Ned, or Sophie to check it over before we open it?" I eyed the brown parcel suspiciously. Big enough to hold a pair of gumboots, addressed to Hazel, my heart started thumping in my chest.

Grandma, it still felt odd thinking of the woman as 'grandma' side eyed me. "We are magic, we are Thornes, we don't need law enforcement." With a flourish of her hands the paper surrounding the item ripped open, revealing a cauldron, like the one that sat on Maz's table. Next to it, something was wrapped in a thick black velvet. "Open it," she gently encouraged me. I crouched next to the package and gently unfolded the material.

A gasp escaped my lips, "Oh Grandma it's beautiful." A ball, made of crystal, clear quartz, judging by the beautiful opaque flecks throughout the sphere, sat on a shiny gold ring.

"They are both yours. Not handed down, these were created with you in mind. I had them commissioned that first week we met. Made in a little village in Scotland where our ancestors lived before migrating. Some of our people are still in that village today." As Hazel moved towards me, I stood and embraced her, making sure the crystal ball wasn't about to roll away. "Both items are made to withstand powerful magic, earthquakes and other freak events." She hugged me tightly. "I'll never be able to make up for all those years where you didn't know who you were, or that your magic was a blessing and not a curse. I will do whatever I can, to guide you to who you are meant to be, who you want yourself to be. Whether you decide on Jane or Clara as your name, you are a powerful witch." Hazel tilted her head thoughtfully. "When we first met, you were Clara to me, now I think Jane fits you better. You are so much more than one or the other."

I tried to speak, but no words came out. I gave Hazel a quick hug, before bending to pick up my gifts. Hazel held out her hand, taking the cauldron through the door to our office, and placing it on my desk. I placed the crystal ball next to it.

My eyes filled with tears at the extent of my grandmother's love. Maybe it didn't matter which name I used. I could be Jane with Hazel and Ned, people who matter to me, and Clara when I want to demonstrate my strength and power. A question for another day, when life settled down. Right now, I was comfortable with Jane.

Our desks were configured to face each other. The door to the office was to my left, and the only window ran the length of the wall on the opposite side to the door. Once we were settled at our desks, my grandmother spoke, "There's no instruction manual for either item. Use your intuition. Books may be useful but know that both magical tools will work for you, because they were made for you. If you have any questions, I'm always here."

A million questions were spinning around in my head. The only one that I managed to verbalise was, "Your mobile that turns into a tablet and provides explanation as to the source of the snow, etc, how is it made?"

Hazel nodded approvingly. I was getting used to understanding her face and body language. "That tablet is several years old. Apparently, the newer versions have an even higher capability for revealing the source of magical anomalies. The technology is created here in the village, by Mikal. When I say, he lives in the village, his home is a cottage, on the outskirts of town. A bunker more than a cottage. He doesn't advertise or leave home often. He's a little paranoid his skills would be hijacked by people with less than noble intentions. Mikal won't talk about it, but he used to work in the city, for a large electronics company." She stared at her hands, and I sensed there was more to Mikal than she was willing to share with us. "He must stay hidden, especially with people like Roberto lurking around. We can't even tell Ned where the tech came from. I can contact Mikal tonight, for two laptops. One for the station and one here. I've a feeling it will come in handy." Hazel turned on her computer. "Now let's get some work done."

Hazel made notes on the notebook beside her keyboard. It was clear question time was over, and I'd learn no more about Mikal. I opened the first of several new emails that sat waiting in my inbox. I'd expected questions about waste collection, annual events, or road closures. Not today. The emails, addressed to Hazel and I were from Robbie Banks. "Unbelievable," I muttered to myself as I opened them, one by one.

"He's persistent," commented my grandmother. The same emails sat in her inbox, asking us for a meeting to discuss in detail his plans for the village. The emails contained a detailed project plan including the address of the sites he'd planned to develop.

"Are all the parcels of land he identifies owned by his company or others? Is any of it still council land? That would make a difference, wouldn't it?" I wasn't exactly sure how these things worked.

No, yes, and not exactly," Hazel responded, as she referred to the list of properties provided by our anonymous visitor. "Some of the land Florence and her in-laws bought years ago, others Robbie has bought, the rest is council land. We can still refuse development, on land owned by residents, if we provide detailed justification of our reasons. We can refuse any development on council land. The problem is, Roberto, Brad, and David could appeal, or get their legal team to tie this up in court for years."

"That'd be bloody minded. If their aim is to make money, lots of it, they wouldn't want to drain their resources. If I wanted to make money and my plans were refused, I'd leave town and look elsewhere." I crossed my fingers, hoping my assessment would prove correct.

"I hope that's true," my grandmother sounded doubtful. "Brad and David are lawyers, and the three of them are bloody minded. Robbie clearly hates that you've bested him once and won't easily let you do so again. He's got no direct magic of his own, but those Hartly brothers do, and I wager they know some magic criminal types who'd be happy to cause havoc."

We sat in silence, letting that thought sink in. I had a bad feeling about what was going to happen next.

"All we can do, is our job," Hazel broke the silence a few minutes later. "We have a council of seven, including us. Let's do the right thing and put it to a vote. I've heard from the others. They've all recovered from their mystery illnesses. I'll set up a meeting for first thing in the morning. I've attached all the application forms, and notes from our meetings with the applicants, to the email invitations." Her fingers flew across her keyboard. "Can you please print off copies of all the information you've found on Roberto, Robbie and anything relevant on the Hartly brothers. I'm assuming you can still access your sources and knowledge from your time as a private investigator."

My energy buzzed around my body. Not nerves, but positive energy, working with family, my grandmother. Understanding that my powers were positive and not something to run and hide from. I was determined not to let anyone spoil my newfound happiness "Not a problem, I'll have packs printed out for all of us."

"The further I dig into the web of lies and deception they've built around their corporations, the more I dislike Brad, David, David and Roberto. It's like they are still weaving the story, changing it slightly the more people like Sophie and I investigate them," I told Ned hours later, as we sat at my kitchen table. "Roberto is the worst offender. He's been arrested several times and has been bankrupted as well. Robbie appears to be an upstanding citizen, and successful businessman with no criminal convictions. If you have enough money, you can make anything look real."

"If you share what you have with Sophie, she may be able to find the anomaly that might send them to gaol." Ned added, "She's a whizz with computers, and we have access to a range of secret databases."

"I'll do that now," I said as I tapped at my keyboard. "When I looked a few days ago, Roberto disappeared around the time Robbie Banks started his businesses. Only several days later, they've re-written the data, so it looks like both men exist at the same time. Which we know is rubbish," I sighed, hoping that working together with the police we'd be able to stop Roberto and the others.

"Thanks so much for dinner, home cooked is the best." Ned placed his knife and fork on his empty plate. "I live on takeaways or microwave meals. I look forward to our dinner dates, for the food and the company," as he smiled, his cheeks reddened.

I managed to keep my cheeks their normal colour as I agreed with the sentiment. "I love the chance to cook for you, and the company." The snow had all but disappeared and the weather had returned to its summery warmth. The pumpkin soup and crusty bread, both made from scratch, had both proved easier to prepare than they sounded.

"Caramel slice and coffee, or hot chocolate?" I asked as I took the plates to the sink.

"Oh yes please. Hot chocolate sounds nice," Ned grinned. "Next time I could cook for you, or we could eat out."

"We could, but I honestly don't mind cooking here, and besides, Sprinkles loves visitors," I chuckled as my pup decided to try to land in Ned's lap.

He patted the pup on the head. "I love that you have the pets. I had to rehome my Barney, it wasn't fair on him, as I was never home. If you don't mind my company, I love coming over here." Barney, a mixed breed rescue dog had been Ned's companion for a few years. A few months ago, he made the painful decision to let him go to live on a farm, with space to run, and a family with children to play with.

Sprinkles sat contentedly beside Ned. Cinnamon walked past his other side, leaving light coloured fluff on his navy trousers. Bert chirped happily. "It looks like they're equally as happy with the arrangement." I slid two large mugs of steaming cocoa onto the table, adding a plate of slice and a couple of serviettes to catch any crumbs.

Ned yawned as he drained the last of his drink. "I'm glad the snow disappeared of its own accord, and that we received no calls of weather-related incidents. If you don't mind, I'm heading home for an early night. The week's not over yet."

"Of course I don't mind, I think the Hartly's have planned more magic displays to distract us. We can catch up for a cuppa tomorrow sometime. Get Sophie to contact me if she needs any additional information." I walked Ned to the door, Sprinkles and Cinnamon followed us. As I touched Ned's arm by way of goodnight, he leant in and pecked me on the cheek, taking me by surprise. I wanted to reciprocate, but Ned was already at his car. I settled for blowing a kiss as he waved.

I'd not felt like this for many years. Ned and I clicked from the first time we met. The village kept throwing us together to solve mysteries. Magic. I let my cheeks flush as I closed the door and headed through to tidy the kitchen. I glanced into my snug. If I moved my cozy arm chair a little, I could squeeze in a small two-seater lounge. "Perfect for snuggling with a handsome policeman," I whispered to my pets, who were flanked either side of me.

Chapter Fifteen

The beeping of my mobile roused me from a dream where Ned and I snuggled together on a cute blue sofa. My mobile told me two things – that it was only 6am and that my grandmother was calling.

I fumbled the phone before managing to press the correct button. "Hazel, are you okay?"

"Jane, apologies for waking you so early. I'm fine, but you'd better turn on the news, and the kettle, I'll be over as soon as I feed Esmerelda." My grandmother's cat was old, grey, and larger than my terrier dog. Visiting my grandmother's house was the only time my pup sat still, refusing to leave my side.

I pulled on my jeans, a fresh shirt, and brushed my unruly hair. I turned on the television news, and the kettle. As I listened to the morning news show I plated up my pet's morning meals and placed two peppermint tea bags into cups.

A sleepy little village in the middle of Australia will be brought to life by local entrepreneur brothers Brad and David Hartly and Robbie Banks when they build a state-of-the-art entertainment centre in the centre of town. The businessmen's plans include other exciting projects, which will inject some much-needed funds into the village. Alongside the entertainment centre and amusement park there are plans to build a brand new fifty room motel, with restaurants, a pool, exercise room, bar and conference centre. After the break we'll interview the men behind this initiative.

"This isn't good," I muttered as I opened the back door for Cinnamon and Sprinkle to spend their allotted time outside. It'll be much harder to refuse the application once it was plastered all over the news as a fait accompli. "I hope Grandma knows a good lawyer," I told Bert as I gently patted his feathers.

I opened my front door as I heard a commotion outside. "Buckets and bilgewater," my elderly next door neighbour Margo exclaimed as I stepped outside. "Did you see the morning news? I'll pack up and leave town before they build that monstrosity here!" She shook her fist as Hazel stepped out of her jeep.

"Come in for a cuppa," I suggested, attempting to calm my neighbour. Hazel steered Margo inside as the advertisements ended and the screen filled with an image of Barbara. The reporter was dressed elegantly in a long black dress, holding the microphone in front of the three men dressed in long sleeved blue shirts and dark jeans. Cowboy hats on their heads, the sun behind them, the men grinned straight into the camera. I dragged my gaze away and poured water into the two cups. I gave one to each of my visitors, foregoing mine, so I didn't miss a second of the ridiculous interview.

My mind wandered, wondering where Barbara and her cameraman were staying whilst in Misty Vale. Last time they reported on our village, when Florence invited them to report on the Christmas characters roaming around town, I assumed she paid them. Brad probably donated money to the television station, to make sure Barbara and Nicholas stayed around to report whenever they were asked to. I made a mental note to investigate the local accommodation to see if they were owned by Brad or David.

"Can you tell us your plans for Misty Vale? Why choose this little village for the site of your million-dollar development?" The reporter pushed her microphone in front of the man in the middle.

Robbie smiled his evil fake smile, his shiny white teeth glistening in the early morning light. He motioned to the man on either side. "When my good friends and business partners Brad and David told me about the untapped potential of the area, I had to come and see it for myself. I've known the brothers for years, since we were at university together." We watched in disbelief as the three men posed and smiled for the audience. Robbie and Brad had darkish short hair, combed strategically to cover balding spots. David's hair was lighter. I wasn't sure which brother was older, though if I had to guess I'd pick Brad. Florence's late husband had been the eldest of the three Hartly brothers. I shuddered, as Robbie continued to spout the benefits of the new enterprise and how it would enhance our town.

"How dare they!" Margo shook her fist at the screen. She turned to Hazel. "What are you doing about it?" The anger in her voice abated a little as she faced off my grandmother.

Hazel drew herself up to her full height. Both women were a little shorter than me. Margo more slightly built of the two. "Jane and I are meeting with the five other members of council first thing this morning to discuss the development applications. We will be discussing our options and which development applications to approve. We still need to meet with those three, and we'll probably ask Barbara for an interview, to clarify things and refute any false claims." Hazel gulped what was left of her tea and placed her empty cup on the side table.

"I'm helping Ned and Sophie to source information about Robbie and the Hartly brothers. If we can prove they have criminal records, have been charged with fraud, or declared bankruptcy we'll have a stronger case to refuse them." I turned to Hazel. "Do you think any of the council members could have already been compromised? I remember Cindy and Mindy offering our residents incentives to vote for Florence. I wouldn't put anything past Robbie and the Hartlys."

"I'm not sure, but that's on the agenda when we meet this morning. I've blocked out the whole morning to finalise this one way or another. I've our solicitor standing by." She paced around my snug, Sprinkles followed, his tail wagging, thinking my grandmother was after a game. Cinnamon watched from her pink cushion. "Something like this happened years ago, before you were born," she told me. It wasn't the Hartlys back then, but another threat."

My neighbour jumped again. "I remember," Margo spoke loudly, startling Sprinkles. "You did a good job, getting rid of those charlatans," she said begrudgingly to Hazel. "Didn't you raise a veil of protection around the village, saving it from con men like these slime buckets, from entering and destroying our mojo?"

I cleared my throat to hide my smile. I tried to steer Margo towards a chair, worried she might have a fall.

"I did weave a strong protection spell, that stayed in place until Cindy and Mindy returned to town." I breathed a sigh of relief at my grandmother's words, worried it might have been my return that caused the problem. "It wasn't your return," Hazel added, touching my arm reassuringly.

"Right, well then, it sounds like you have it all under control." Margo handed me her empty cup. "Thank you for my tea. I'm going to talk to my plants." My neighbour loved her garden, her green thumb well known throughout the village.

"I'll call in later this afternoon," I said as I led her to the door. I knew she'd grumble if I offered her any assistance to get back through her gate.

Hazel had rinsed the cups and was patting both my pets as I returned to the kitchen. "Do you need to do anything else before we head out?" she asked.

I glanced around the room. The animals had been fed, they could wander outside via the cat flap, Bert had seed and water. "I've got to slip on shoes, grab my laptop and my handbag and we're good to go." I was thankful I'd chosen a fresh dress shirt when I'd hastily dressed earlier. I picked up my hairbrush and a large clip, man handling my hair into a bun as I followed Hazel to her jeep.

Customers milled in line at the café. Jess had her elvin helpers making the coffee and preparing the toasties and muffins. Barbara and

Nicholas were huddled at a table by the door. "I want to talk to you," my grandmother marched up to their table, wagging her finger at the blonde. "Can you please provide me the name and contact detail for your boss? I'm considering suing the media outlet you work for, for misrepresenting the truth. The village has not agreed to any monstrous development or business plan. The council is meeting this morning to discuss the applications."

I lined up to place our order, positioning myself so I could still hear the conversation. The reporter spluttered a little but recovered well. "I'll not give you the name of my editor, but I'll be available to interview you, at 1pm this afternoon."

It would be easy to find her editors details. Hazel probably knew that. "Come by the council office at 12:45pm," Hazel countered, turning her back, dismissing the reporter.

"Good morning, Jane, Hazel. I'm guessing you saw the news, like everyone else in the village. I'm so pleased I've extra helpers this morning to cater to the additional foot traffic. Your order will be ready soon."

"Thanks Jess, a large latte and a large mocha, two toasted sandwiches, and two lemon drizzle muffins please," I smiled as Jess scribbled the order. I watched as the young blonde teens efficiently created drinks and plated up the orders, not fazed by the volume of customers.

Hazel leant in towards Jess. "I probably don't have to tell you, but the interview was all lies. The council are meeting this morning. If you feel like letting your customers know this information, well that would be great." she added with a smile.

"Anything I can do, to help stop the craziness of the Hartlys count me in," Jess said fiercely. "I'm fourth generation in the village and the thought of it being turned into a tourist attraction turns my stomach," She paused, as one of her helpers passed a range of items towards her. "Now, here you go, drinks and food. Good luck." Jess smiled at us, before turning her attention to the customer waiting behind us.

We quickly walked the short distance to the office. "I considered ordering in cuppas and muffins for the meeting, but I don't want to be seen to be coercing anyone, offering brides," Hazel commented as I held open the door for her.

"It's sad that it's come to that, but yes I agree one hundred percent." I set our breakfasts on our desks. "Do you mind if I send the information to the printer and swot up on the members of council. I don't think I've met any of them face to face."

"Go for it. We have a couple of hours. I've set up the room next door as the meeting place, it has a bigger table in the middle of the room, so we don't have to move furniture around." Hazel opened her laptop. "All you need to know about the other council members is – John is an earth elemental, Joan is water, Sharon is fire, Steve is air, and Bill is non-magical. They've all been on council for years, Steve, Sharon and Bill joined the council after I stepped down. Joan and John were descendants of previous council members. While it's not a hereditary role, we tend to find family members are more interested in stepping up than others, though that may have changed now."

The next couple of hours passed mostly in silence as my grandma and I ate breakfast and planned for the meeting. Was Hazel feeling anxious? Returning to the leadership role she left so long ago. Did anxiety run in the family? I breathed through the fear of failure trying expel my breakfast from my stomach.

"Are there any members you think we should pay close attention to? Do you suspect anyone may be supporting Brad and the others?" I asked as we waited in the large meeting room, for the others to arrive.

"They are at the same time, all trustworthy and open to bribery." Hazel paced back and forth in front of the door. "Their families are multigenerational to the village." She stopped, mid-sentence and stride as voices floated down the corridor. She slipped on a welcoming smile as the councillors shuffled in. Joan was a little taller than Hazel, of slight build, with short black hair in a bob style cut. Steve and Sharon were around my height, John and Bill were closer to six feet tall. They all wore jeans and a bright green top with the name of our village blazoned across the back. Their first names embroidered on the front of their polo shirts. I wondered the occasion that decided these shirts were the council uniform.

Hazel spoke as soon as the last person, John, found a vacant chair. "Good morning and thank you all for coming along. Let's make a start, we've a lot to talk about." She motioned to where I sat, opposite her at the rectangular table. "I'd like you all to meet my granddaughter. Clara, or Jane as she has been known by since arriving in the village. It's helpful for her that you all appear to have your names in prominent sight," she smiled, though I could tell she wasn't a fan of their attire.

The group mumbled "Good morning," as they joined us at the table.

Sharon sat to my left. "We volunteer at the local market days, sporting events, and the annual festival. We wanted to stand out, so people would know who to go to if they needed assistance." She proudly patted her green shirt. "We can order you both shirts, we'll just need to confirm sizes, and whether you want Clara or Jane on yours." Sharon smiled at me.

I tried not to grin too widely as I replied, "I think the shirts are perfect for being seen in a crowd."

John coughed to draw attention, then leant forward. "Before we start, you need to know that Joan and I have been approached by Mr Banks and the Hartly brothers. We were offered incentives if we vote for their business. Fairly large incentives."

Bill held his hand up. "We've all been contacted."

I made notes on the open page of my notebook. I kicked myself that I hadn't run background checks for each of the people in the room. I'd planned to, but it slipped my mind. "How did you respond to their offer?" I took the lead, sensing my grandmother was reading auras, and detecting lies. When no one immediately responded I added, "It's our business only if you're a member of the council. If you resign, then any deals struck between yourself, and another party is technically none of our concern. Unless one of the parties has been previously convicted of fraud, bankruptcy etc. I assume you are savvy enough to have completed background checks to assure yourself of the integrity of their business offer."

It didn't take an aura reading to pick who'd either taken up the offer or was considering doing so. A quick glance at Hazel confirmed the accuracy of my assessment. Hazel frowned around the table. "One of our urgent matters today is to vote on whether to approve a series of development applications submitted by Mr Banks and the Hartlys. Bill, John, I trust you are going to excuse yourselves, and hand in resignation letters. By the end of the day please." It was clear my grandmother wasn't giving them an option.

Bill stood first. Over six feet tall, and still broad shouldered, he held his advancing years well. His hat advertising his goat farm covered what hair remained on his head. I'd heard of *Goats Abound!* I wanted to try some of the goat's milk soaps created onsite. "Sorry Hazel, the farm could do with the added funds, and I couldn't refuse the offer to sell the products in shops in the bigger towns and cities. They have connections I could never find myself."

"I understand, you have to do what's right for you," Hazel replied, though her tone made it clear she didn't approve. "Goodbye Bill, please leave your resignation on my desk, and email a copy through." The goat farmer bowed his head, and walked around the table, past the others to exit the room. Hazel turned to face John. "Well?"

The younger man's face flushed as he fidgeted in his chair. "You need me on council," he said petulantly. "I'm connected. You think you can return to your role and change things that have been working for years."

"It's simple John. If you take up their offer, you can't sit on council. I understand your farm may need a boost and they've told you they can help. Are you working with them or not?"

"It's not easy making money on a farm that sells seasonal flowers, even for an earth elemental," he continued to whine. "The family needs me to make the right decisions. Brad told us he'll get our products in all the best shops in the city. He's going to recommend our flowers for all types of corporate events and celebrations."

"I wouldn't for a moment suggest you don't make the right decisions for your family. You will conduct your own due diligence. My only stipulation is if you work with the developers, you no longer sit on this council." My grandmother stood and motioned for John to leave.

All eyes stared at John, following him as he eventually stood and exited the room, slamming the door shut behind him. Sharon got up and reopened the door.

Hazel looked around the room. "Does anyone else have to declare an interest in the proceedings?" Murmurs of 'no' met her questioning gaze. She nodded to me.

"I hope you've had time to read and think about the proposals and your position on each of them. We'll discuss each application separately. Hazel and I want to hear your views, before we offer ours. Are there any questions or comments before we start discussions and voting?" I passed out printed copies of the information previously sent to their email addresses.

Sharon placed her hands on the table and faced Hazel. "I have one question. Are you here for good this time? If Jane leaves town, or something else happens, will you still retain the role that is your birthright?" Her deep brown eyes stared into my grandmother's equally deep green-brown eyes.

Hazel held her gaze. "I am here to stay. There's no point apologising for the past. I'm here to fulfill my role, to ensure Misty Vale is safe for its residents and that no one creates a circus or a spectacle of our haven."

By 12:30pm we'd managed to discuss the proposals and cast our votes. None of applications put forward by Brad, David, and Robbie were successful. Of the other applications we'd received, Tricia's nursery and Casey's woodworking project received unanimous approval to go ahead.

"I understand the council has a grants fund available for use at our discretion." Hazel caught the eye of each of us around the table. "I recommend we offer a one-off grant to both applicants. I'm not suggesting we dissuade them from taking advantage of any offers they may receive from Brad, but I'd like us to support them. They're local, and their businesses are beneficial to our village."

The remaining councillors looked at each other and slowly raised their hands.

Sharon spoke first, "I agree with your idea. It sounds like a good use of council grants money." The other two nodded their agreement. "When you let the applicants know they're successful, please ask them to fill in the appropriate form. It's on the council website."

I tapped on my keyboard and found the relevant form. "Thanks Sharon. I'll contact Casey and Tricia today and ask them to do so." I glanced at Hazel. "I'll contact the unsuccessful people too. I guess we should speak to Brad, David and Robbie in person. They won't be impressed that we made the decision without hearing them out." I winced at the thought of those conversations.

"I was willing to meet them, until they pulled that publicity stunt this morning. I'd scheduled meetings for this afternoon. After waking up to the news report, I'm not interested in having an audience with them." I felt the anger and annoyance in Hazel's voice. It remained stern as she addressed the others. "If they try to contact you, it's up to you how you deal with that, but my thoughts are you decline to enter a conversation. The decision made here today is final."

"What about the media? That reporter lady was hovering around the building earlier." Joan asked, fiddling with her handbag.

"You leave Barbie to me." I chuckled at Hazel's nickname for our blonde bombshell reporter, who resembled a certain popular doll. I've scheduled an interview with her, in…" Hazel checked her watch, "…ten minutes. I'll bring her up to speed on what the council have decided and give her the opinion to formally detract the earlier interview. I'll speak to her editor afterwards, to make sure we are on the same page."

"Thank you, Hazel, I'm glad you are back. Jane, I'm glad you're here too." Sharon's snow-white hair sat neatly around her face, accentuating her blue eyes. "I kept all the records during the last thirty odd years. You'll find paper copies in the filing cabinet in your office. I'll send you a link to where they are stored electronically."

"Thank you, Sharon," I responded as Hazel gathered her things. "I'd like to suggest we reconvene same time tomorrow morning, to deal with any fall out from today. Also, it will be a chance to get to know each other a little better."

"Can we bring coffee and cake?" Joan asked.

I glanced at my grandmother. She nodded her agreement. "Yes, let's do that. Have a great afternoon, and we'll chat more tomorrow." I rose, as did Hazel. The others took the hint and followed us out.

"Please join me," Hazel said quietly as we approached our office. Barbie and her cameraman were already hovering in the corridor. I suspected they'd been inside the office, unaware of the cloaking spell that would render useless any search for information.

With a subtle move of her hand, three chairs were set up in the space between our desks. "You sit there," Hazel pointed the reporter to a chair. She gave the cameraman a glance that told him to do whatever he needed to, as we took out seats opposite.

Hazel let Barbie introduce her 'informal chat with self-appointed mayor of Misty Vale, Hazel Thorne'. She shot her a withering look before taking the microphone and facing the camera. "My role as mayor is not self-appointed. It's an obligation tied into a family ancestry that we don't have time to explain that detail in this interview. If you are interested, I can provide that information afterwards. The purpose of this chat is to correct an earlier inaccurate interview with Robbie Banks, Brad and David Hartly." She paused for effect. "Misty Vale council has voted unanimously against the business applications received by those three businessmen. The applicants have been notified via email." I nodded slightly, to confirm I'd pressed send on the emails I'd drafted during the earlier discussion. "If you hear any information contrary to this, know that it is not true."

The reporter leant towards Hazel, "What do you think the repercussions will be? What happens to the village if the projects don't go ahead?"

Hazel stared down the lens. "We'll survive. More than that, our villagers are quite capable of looking after ourselves."

Barbie touched the earpiece in her ear. "What about the two councillors who resigned? Did you even have enough people to hold the meeting?"

"We had a quorum," Hazel said firmly. "We'll be approaching the community for nominations to replace the outgoing members," she added before the reporter could ask.

"Do you expect any negative response to your decision? Not all the villagers agree that it is in their best interest not to have progress." Barbie tried to sound sincere, showing concern for the community.

"I see no problem with progress, but a gaudy circus of an entertainment centre that makes a mockery of our residents, and an amusement themed holiday accommodation aren't sensible steps forward," Hazel responded firmly. "Our residents aren't easily tricked by offers of shiny things."

Barbie turned her attention to me. "And you, Jane, or would you prefer Clara? What are your long-term plans? Are you planning on running away, like your parents did?"

My anger seethed below the surface. I felt it in every fibre of my being as I clenched and unclenched my fists. I couldn't look at Hazel, but

I heard her voice, in my head. *Calm down, focus your energy.* I didn't want to blast the room apart, or to send the weather haywire.

"I'm not my parents. I've no plans to ever leave Misty Vale. Still, I'd be a fool to say I'll be here forever. No one knows what the future holds," I spoke firmly. "What I know is, I'll be doing whatever is within my power to help keep Misty Vale the magical safe place it has been for over one hundred years." I leant forward. "Why are you here Barbara? Are you interested in reporting the truth, or are you being paid to skew the information?" I took a risk, knowing the reporter didn't have to respond, or keep the camera rolling.

While the reporter tried to think of a response, my grandmother spoke, "As we navigate through this, I suggest you and I meet daily."

Barbie turned to Hazel, a mix of surprise and horror evident on her face. "Why?"

"So that we can make sure we tell the public what is really happening, and not an untrue version of events." My grandmother stood. "As there are no more questions, let's finish for today, and reconvene tomorrow." She held the door open and waited for the reporter and cameraman to leave. "That went well," she said as she closed the door behind them.

I wasn't entirely sure whether Hazel's words were sarcastic. "Better than I thought it would," I acknowledged. "Now we wait and see what happens. I'm sure there'll be fall out, from our decisions and the interview." Hazel and I returned the chairs to their place at our desks. I opened my laptop. Half a dozen emails waited for me.

"I'm assuming you have the email from Robbie," Hazel said from behind her computer. "Threatening to sue us for goodness knows what."

"From Brad and David as well, reading them now," I murmured as I scanned the words in front of me. "Yep, they're using words like 'defamation of character' and 'broken contracts.' A couple of threatening sentences thrown in for good measure."

"I see. Please don't reply to any of the emails. I'll deal with them," she said firmly. "Why don't you go and get us some food. Lunch, or afternoon tea. See if Ned's free to catch up. I'm contacting our lawyer. And don't stress."

Chapter Sixteen

The option not to stress, was as foreign to me as a loving family, and good friends. *No, that was the old me, Jane Fairweather. I'm Clara Thorne, weaver of magic, and member of a founding family of Misty Vale.* I told myself as I stretched my legs. The main street was surprisingly quiet.

I sent Ned a message, *Coffee and cake, at the café?*

Ned responded straight away, *Five minutes.*

By the time he arrived, I'd order us coffees and a couple of Jess's new cupcakes. A cherry and chocolate Misty Vale Cheer. "Named in honour of our amazing village," she beamed as she showed off her new creations. "I'm working on some more mystical, magic themed cupcakes in preparation for our celebration."

"I can't wait to try them." Ever since I walked into the café on that first day, when I hopped off the touring coach, I fell in love with Jess's culinary creations. Minty, citrus, berries, there were too many flavours of cupcakes for me to choose a favourite.

"You've had a busy morning," Ned commented as he sat on the seat opposite mine. "I've had Brad Hartly on the phone asking me to arrest you and your grandmother. He suggested I could be creative and invent some crime to convict you of. Having a conviction would mean no longer serving on the council."

My anger fumed, but I quickly got it under control. "I'm tempted to ring him and tell him exactly what I think of him. I won't," I reassured the policeman, "I don't want to give him the satisfaction."

Ned sipped his caramel latte. "Nice flavours," he commented, "And don't worry, I gave him a talking to for trying to waste police time and tying up our resources. He back pedalled, I thought he was going to apologise for a moment. He doesn't want any bad publicity. He didn't realise he couldn't buy our police support."

I savoured the sweet taste of the caramel syrup in my coffee. The cupcake flavours exploded in my mouth. It may be my new favourite, even more so than the jaffa cupcake, another of Jess's creations. "I thought the drink and cake would give us both a boost for the rest of the day. I'm taking some back to Hazel as well. She hasn't stopped since early morning. Apart from Brad making a fuss, has it been quiet at the station?"

"Not a quiet day, no. A lot of walk ins and calls about magic being used illegally. We investigated each occurrence but found no evidence of criminal activity." Ned bit into his mini cake. "This is delicious."

"Do you think it's the same as last time, when Florence and the others caused magical mayhem to distract from what they were really up to?" I polished off my cupcake and contemplated another.

"It feels a little like that. Last time they had us running around town, chasing down haywire magic, while they tried to coerce the founding families to give up their magic." Ned popped the last bit of cake into his mouth. I sensed he was trying to piece together what was behind the latest spate of incidents. "This time I think they are trying to prove our village magic is out of control. That we need assistance to teach people how to use their powers. Which is absolute nonsense."

"Do you think Robbie and the Hartlys could be trying to run you and Sophie around so much, or prove you can't solve the crimes, so they can replace you with police who'll get rid of Hazel and me? Does that sound paranoid? I'm trying to think like them." Ned raised his eyebrows, so I added. "I've worked on so many cases, in the police force and as a private investigator, I tend to be able to tap into how a criminal mind works."

Ned drank the rest of his latte while he considered my thoughts. "It's possible. I wouldn't put anything past those three. I wonder if the computer programme Hazel has could determine whether a crime was legit or a wild goose chase?" He shook his head ruefully, "Nah, that'd be too easy."

"I'll ask her. I want to work on my magic, my intuition and reading people. If we could prove our businessmen were less than noble, we could have them arrested. Or force them to leave town. Unless they have high powered solicitors or judges in their employ. Sorry for being melodramatic, it's so lovely here, it feels like home, and I dread the thought that anyone can destroy it, or that I'll have to leave again."

Ned looked up in surprise. "You wouldn't leave, would you?"

I reached across and touched his hand for a few seconds. "I'm not planning on going anywhere, well except for back to the office, with coffee and cake for Hazel." My eyes locked with his, sending pleasant tingles through my body. "If you get a chance, I should be home by 6pm if you'd like dinner."

Before Ned could answer his mobile beeped shrilly. "I'll let you know," he rose to his feet, phone to his ear as he left the café. I picked up the coffee and cake for Hazel, and a couple of extra cakes. I mouthed my thanks to Jess, as she was busy with a family of four, a large rainbow cake and balloons.

Hazel looked up from her computer screen as I entered. "Oh good, you caught up with Ned, I take it."

I placed two cakes and her cup in front of her, taking the last cake to my laptop. "I did. He's been having a difficult time. Certain businessmen have been asking for you and I to be arrested or run out of town. When he refused, suddenly they're being called out to a lot of bogus crime incidents. It's driving them crazy."

"Oh, have they now?" Hazel drew herself up to her full height, seated, as she took a long drink of her latte. "It's a good thing I'm meeting with Leopold later this afternoon. Our lawyer and long-time family friend," she added by way of explanation.

"Would you like me to be there?" I asked, scrolling through the emails in my inbox.

"Not this time, thank you, but I'd like to introduce you to him soon."

I remembered Ned's question. "While I think of it, would Mikal be able to add a component to the software to allow Ned and Sophie to tell if a crime was bogus or legitimate?"

"I'll have a word to him. It may be possible, after all we can tell if an incident has magic connected to it." Hazel looked at the cupcakes in front of her. "We'll be bouncing off the walls, with such a sugar over-load."

I looked at my now empty cupcake case. "Yeah, sorry about that, I'd planned on getting us chicken salad wraps, but I got distracted."

"By a tall handsome policeman, I'll wager." My grandmother caused my cheeks to flush. It was hot in the office. I glanced at my empty water bottle.

A loud knock on the office door distracted my thoughts. "You'd better come and see this." Without waiting for an answer, Sharon strode off towards the front of the building. Outside a crowd had formed around the reporter and cameraman, who'd set up a makeshift studio in the front room of the building next door.

The vacant building next to our office had been during various stages, a fish and chip shop, a solicitor's office, and a playgroup. In the last few hours, it'd been transformed into the headquarters of the Banks and Hartly Developments. According to the flash new sign and window dressing. I heard my grandmother behind me. I felt her anger, simmering, I didn't need to turn around. I reached back and held her fingers.

Bill and John were seated on a comfortable dark blue lounge. Lighting and sound gear were arranged, creating a semi-permanent interview space. In a room off to the right I saw Brad, David, and Robbie seated on plush leather chairs at old heavy wooden desks. The site oozed opulence. Their position, in plain view through the glass windows, indicated they wanted to be seen.

I wiggled my toes, to dissipate my energy. I felt the familiar telltale rising of my emotions, my energy, that spark that triggered explosions of my magic. Now wasn't the time to let my emotions get the better of me. I suspected Hazel would need as much level headedness as I could muster. Although she didn't appear to be seventy years old, she'd been out of the public eye for over thirty years. Her decision to step away from the leadership role had been more about family and perception than anxiety. I didn't want a couple of bullies and reporters to send her back to her cottage and her grumpy old cat.

A few steps to our left, I gently steered Hazel to a strategic position. We could see Bill and John, and if I concentrated, I might be able to hear Robbie's discussion. About twenty onlookers had made their way into the building, to listen to the interview. Two big screens were erected on poles in the street. The crowd had grown in the few minutes since our arrival.

"It's awfully short sighted of Hazel and her granddaughter, to dismiss Bill and I, on the basis that we want to grow our businesses. Robbie Banks is new to Misty Vale, but if Brad and David vouch for him, he's okay in my book." John stared intensely into the camera.

Bill fidgeted on his side of the lounge. "John and I have dedicated years to the village. We've never been involved in any crime or committed fraud. Having the opportunity to be a part of an exciting new project in the village should be something we can all look forward to."

My fingers tightened around Hazel's as the reporter asked John and Bill what they're plans were. Both rushed to confirm their eagerness to grow their businesses with the help of Brad and the others. Their farms would in turn, continue to support the village I tuned into the muted voices in the next room. "If enough people continue to support us, we'll easily get rid of Hazel and Jane." Robbie's voice was little louder than a whisper, still I heard it, clear as if I were in front of him. Confirmation of my growing powers. I turned, my back towards the businessmen, I didn't need to see them to know I was eavesdropping.

A few seconds later I felt a rough hand on the small of my back. I swung around and nearly bumped into Roberto's large nose. "Get your hand off me," I hissed.

"You and your grandmother need to leave now, or do we need to call on the local police force to remove you?" He said loudly enough that heads turned towards us. "This building is private property." He puffed out his chest. Standing toe to toe with my nemesis didn't worry me. He was no taller than I and was all bluff and bluster.

I turned away from my detractor and linked my arm with Hazel's. Without another word, I lead her through the front door and out into the street. Instead of heading straight back into the office, I led her in the opposite direction, through a side alleyway and into our building by the back door.

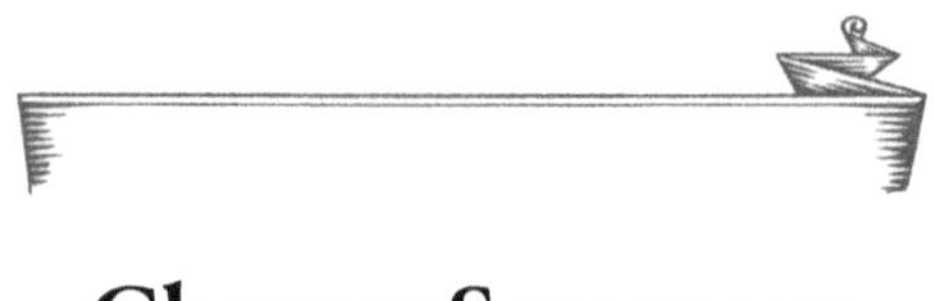

Chapter Seventeen

"That's a fine how-do-you," Hazel sounded fiery as she plonked herself back into her desk chair. I side-eyed her with concern. She wasn't as young as she appeared. I didn't know what happened when she got upset, or angry and I wasn't keen on finding out

"Shall I make us a couple of teas? Or pour us some fresh water?" I suggested, not exactly sure how I was feeling. Angry, indignant, a little fearful and anxious if I tried to be honest. My overriding emotion was the desire to protect my grandmother.

"Tea and water would be perfect," Hazel agreed. "Don't you be worried about me, I'm not about to melt into a blubbering mess," she deadpanned. "I want to write down some thoughts while they are fresh in my head, if you don't mind."

I swallowed the lump in my throat; her tone belied her emotions. Upset, betrayed, exhausted. I felt them all as if they were mine. I opened my mouth to say something, but Hazel's bowed head as she wrote in her notebook didn't invite conversation. I left my grandmother and made two peppermint teas and glasses of water in the kitchenette. A long thin room complete with a pantry, a full-size refrigerator, oven, stove top, and microwave. The women who used to work there, used the kitchenette to prepare lunch and teas during nine-hour shifts. Back in the day when they could bring their children to work. I knew there was several offices in the old building. A couple of community clubs used the space, a mother's club, and indoor handmade markets sometimes set up inside. My feet led me into a big open space, the area in the building that was previously used as a creche. It still contained a few pieces of child sized furniture.

I headed back to our office with our drinks on a tray, an idea forming in my mind. "How did the current council come to be formed? When you stepped down, were there nominations, an election? I assume the leadership has something to do with founding families?"

Hazel took her cup of tea and glass of water, peering at me over her glasses. "As far as I know, yes, the founding families had representatives on the council. Once I stepped down Florence was more vocal than the others, they let her run things and tell them what to do. The original intent was the founding family members, with their elemental magic, were stewards, or guardians, using their combined powers to keep us safe. The council is supposed to work as a unit, with a Thorne as their leader – that's the wrong word, it's more than that."

I patted Hazel's hand. "I understand what you mean. Do you think any of the family members still in the village would be willing to join the council? Would they be more likely to side with the Hartlys?" I took a big drink of my water while Hazel considered my questions.

My grandmother eyed me over the top of her cup, reading my thoughts. "We'd have to ensure the council members joined for the right reasons." She smiled, despite her frustration. "Let me think about it, and we can talk tomorrow morning, before our meeting. Unless something else untoward happens." She glanced at the round clock face that hung above my desk. "It's nearly 4pm. Why don't you head home and try to relax. I'm meeting with Leopold soon, and I want to talk to Mikal afterward."

I moved around to where Hazel sat and hugged her. "Do you promise to eat something? Either with Leopold, Mikal, or when you get home." The last thing I wanted was for my only living relative to get sick because she forgot to look after herself.

"I will and thank you for caring. I may have been sitting at home for a long time, in a hermit like fashion, and I am old," Hazel looked at her upturned palms, "But if needed, I'm still a force to be reckoned with. Are you spending the evening with that handsome young man of yours?" She smiled as she tucked her notebook into her handbag.

This time I kept my cheeks an even colour. "If Ned doesn't get caught up with work, he'll call in later this afternoon."

"Go enjoy yourself, or work on the plan you're hatching in that smart brain on yours." Hazel opened the outer door. "Would you like a lift home?"

I considered the option. The temperature sat in the high thirties, still I felt like walking. "It's only a short distance. I'd like to walk. I may even call into The Crafty Owl. I'm sure there's some craft kit I'd like to buy. I probably should call into the supermarket and pick up something for dinner."

We parted ways at Hazel's jeep. I headed towards the supermarket first. With no idea what food I was going to choose I decided on a selection of cold meats, cheeses, crackers and salad. If Ned couldn't make it, it would simply sit in the fridge for another day.

My skin crawled as I sensed Robbie somewhere within the store. I was tempted to flee the store, instead I marched forcefully, to collect the items I needed. "Ah Jane, or is it Clara now?" Roberto rounded the corner, almost running into me.

"Roberto," I nodded curtly.

"While I didn't expect to find you in Misty Vale, we don't need to be enemies here. I fear we got off on the wrong foot. Can we try again?" He held out his hand.

Ignoring his hand, I walked past Roberto towards the freezer section. Ice cream would be nice for dessert. He followed me. In front of the rows of themed cakes and cupcakes I felt his hot breath on the back of my neck. "If that's how you want to be, then fine, you destroyed my life, my reputation, and my relationships. I'm going to delight in doing the same to you," he hissed. In a normal voice he added cheerily, "It was good to see you, I'm sure we'll meet again soon."

It took all my will power not to bring the shelves of packaged goods down on top of us both. I gripped the handles of the basket. *I am safe* – I repeated the mantra in my head as I forced myself to walk to the freezer doors, pick out a tub of berry swirl confectionery, and walk to the checkout. *I am safe* – I kept the words on a loop as I paid for my items and exited the building. I inhaled the fresh, dry, stifling air as I walked briskly towards the main street.

Cathy waved as I passed The Crafty Owl. I waved back, not feeling like chatting and eager to get home and check on my animals. I jumped as my mobile beeped. With shaking hands, I checked the text. Hazel, letting me know she'd dropped my presents at my house. It seemed days ago that I'd unwrapped the crystal ball and the cauldron. My message back thanked her and warned her that Roberto had threatened me and my family. I hated sending that information in a text, but she needed to know of the threat.

By the time I rounded the corner to my house, Hazel pulled up in her jeep. "Get in, Leopold can wait." We drove the short distance to my cottage in silence. She pulled up out the front but kept the engine running. "Unfortunately, I do have to make that meeting so I can't come in." She pointed to the ring I wore on my right ring finger. "Use your power, through the ring, to create a protection spell. The words will come to you. You can protect your home and your pets." My grandmother paused as she saw the look in my eyes. A mixture of horror, fear, and anxiety. "Don't worry about me. I have an ancient magic running through my veins that I've spent years learning and I've powerful protection wards in place in my house, this jeep, the office. You can protect yourself, surround yourself with a cloak of light that won't let evil penetrate it. It's not as scary as it sounds. Use your intuition. I'm sorry, I do have to go. Message me if you need anything. I'll be here first thing in the morning." She hugged me. I nodded my thanks, not trusting myself not to burst into tears if I spoke.

I sighed with relief that Margo wasn't in her garden. I didn't feel like talking to anyone except my furry family. With the items Hazel left on my front step in my arms, I unlocked my front door. As soon as I crossed the threshold, I locked and bolted the door.

Sprinkles bounded up to greet me, tail wagging excitedly. "Hello boy," I bent to pat my eager pup. "Hi Cinnamon," I added as she wove her body around my jeans legs. "Let's get you fed and watered." I dropped my presents and groceries gently on the floor. Sprinkles sniffed them, until the sound of food dragged him into the kitchen.

Bert chirped his thanks while the others noisily and daintily ate their evening meals. After putting the ice cream in the freezer, cheese, meats and salads in the fridge, and crackers in the cupboard, I looked at the digital clock on the stove. Ned would be an hour away, or longer. I stared at the ring on my finger. The stones glinted, as if the sun shone directly on them. Which it couldn't be doing from where I stood.

The kitchen instinctively felt like the centre of the cottage. The warm glow of the ring told me I was correct. The five stones glowed brightly. In lieu of any written words I spoke aloud those swirling around in my head.

The power of this ring, of my ancestors, protect me and those I hold dear to me. I invoke my powers to join with yours, to ensure no harm comes to me, my animal family, my grandmother, Ned, or any of the friends I've made here.

Was it too much to include my wider friendship circle and the village?

Keep me, Hazel, and my furry and feathered family safe from Roberto and others who would try to hurt us or send us away.

Each of the stones sparkled as I spoke and repeated the word three times. Blue, red, green, purple, orange, each burned brightly one by one, then all together as I ended my spell with the words –

So mote it be.

Where had I heard those words? At Maz's place. It sounded like the correct way to finish the incantation. It was likely my imagination, but a sense of calmness permeated the space. Even my pets seemed quieter than normal. Especially Sprinkles, who'd normally be jumping all over me after I'd been away for so long.

I sighed and smiled tentatively. Home. Hazel. Ned. My powers. Roberto notwithstanding, my life was in much better shape than ever before. The crystals in the ring hummed. I held my hand up to my ear. Their sound felt like sunshine. There was no other way to describe it. I cleared the kitchen table and placed my cauldron and crystal ball on the side I used for craftwork. The old sturdy rectangular table I chose specifically as it was large enough to cut material for sewing, craft, to complete puzzles and still have enough space to sit and eat a meal.

The heavy black cast iron pot. Cold to touch. Did it have a hidden internal power source? What could I use to test it? I rummaged in the top drawer in the tallboy in the snug and found the set of tealight candles I'd bought in case of a blackout. I placed one into the pot. I chuckled out loud. Why did I think placing a candle in the pot would light it? My hand touched the cauldron as I went to retrieve the candle. With a tiny noise I stared in disbelief as the candle lit itself. Did I do that, by touching the cast iron? I popped in another candle. To test my theory. Nothing. I touched the pot. The candle lit up. "That's cool!" I said aloud.

Opening my front door tentatively, I snipped a little of my rosemary and lavender plants. "Let's see if the aroma is released in the pot," I told Sprinkles, as he tried to see what I was up to. Thankfully as he grew older, he no longer jumped on the furniture. It'd be a catastrophe if he burnt his nose on my simmer pot. My feline familiar was too ladylike to jump on the table; she preferred to talk to me from the floor.

As the subtle herb aroma permeated the air I turned my attention to the crystal ball. The metal ring underneath it held it safely in place. About the diameter of a small dessert bowl, the subtle imperfections in the clear quartz caught my eye. "I've no idea how to read this," I told Bert. He chirped conversationally, happy for the interaction. I rubbed my hands softly. I moved them back and forth as if a springy sponge sat between them. Slowly, I moved them towards the ball, as if I were warming them in front of a fire. I stared mesmerised as the crystal started shimmering. I blinked, as the picture in front of me came into focus. I blinked again, concentrating on what the divination tool was trying to tell me. As the image started to clear, an explosion rocked my cottage.

Chapter Eighteen

I grabbed onto the back of the chair in front of me. The crystal ball didn't move but the image it was going to share vanished. I blew out the candles. Bert chirped incessantly, his whole body bobbing up and down. "It's okay Bert." I steadied his cage as it wobbled precariously on its hook. Cinnamon and Sprinkles were huddled together under the table. "You're okay too," I joined them on the floor, rubbed their backs, and reassured them we were safe.

Were we safe? I opened the back door, peering into the backyard. Nothing appeared to be disturbed there. The bathroom, bedroom, spare room, and snug hadn't suffered any damage. I opened the front door, fiddling with the ring on my hand as I did.

"Bells and whistles what was that?" Margo shuffled out of her front door, in slippers and a long flowing kaftan. "I'd just settled into reading my new book, with a cuppa and a box of chocolates."

"Are you okay?" I asked, knowing my question would unleash another string of words. Margo wasn't a bad neighbour, she was lonely, not that she'd ever admit it.

"Okay? Do I sound okay? What's happening around here?" She leant against the wooden fence palings. I was worried she'd fall, although she wasn't much older than my parents, she was stick thin, and seemed older, and frailer than my grandmother.

"Do you want to come in? Or for me to stay with you for a while?" I wanted to know what was going on, but I was willing to make sure my neighbour felt safe.

"No, I do not, just make sure nothing happens, please. You're friends with that policeman, and with Hazel being your grandmother, well, you've got a lot to live up to." She waved me away as she shuffled back through her front door. It shut with a bang behind her.

Margo was right. As Hazel's granddaughter I did have responsibility for the village. Were Hazel and Ned okay? I returned to the kitchen and retrieved my mobile from where I'd left it in my handbag. Four missed messages flashed on the screen.

I'm okay, don't stress. The explosion was the result of someone trying to summon magic. Not their own. I'll explain tomorrow. At least Hazel's message reassured me she was fine. I needed to tune into my intuition more than my anxiety.

I'll be a little late, but I'll be there for dinner if that's still okay. I need your help with something. It wasn't the first time the handsome policeman had seconded me to help with a case.

The message from Maz was a surprise. *Calling a coven meeting tomorrow at 2pm if you can make it.*

The last text, from an unknown number, simply said, *Watch your back.*

I ignored the last text and responded to Maz that if my council meeting was over by two, I'd be there. I messaged Ned that dinner whenever he could make it would be fine. Feeling at a loose end, I turned on the television, in case the explosion had made the news.

I'm reporting live from Misty Vale, where an explosion has rocked the quaint little village. No damage has been found so far, but residents are left wondering, what will happen next.

My breath stuck in my throat. How did the rest of the country, or the world, deal with reports of magic? I exhaled slowly. Barbie hadn't used that word. The news switched to an advertisement of a popular brand of takeaway food available in the bigger towns. The news programme returned to the studio, where the man sitting at the desk apologised for the previous footage. He explained it wasn't meant to make it to air, and it certainly wasn't live. Barbie didn't strike me as someone who'd like her credibility questioned. I smiled to myself. Grandmother must have spoken to the journalist's superiors.

Did Brad, or Robbie set up that news bulletin, to cause more controversy? News like that tended to drive visitors towards the events. I threw my hands up in disgust. Balls of wool flew out of the basket. Rising up in the air, they landed on the floor without damaging anything. "It's lucky I don't collect sharp objects," I said with a laugh.

I returned to the crystal ball. I'd not caused the explosion, trying to use my new tool had I? No. Grandmother would have said. I shook my head. *It's time I trusted my intuition;* I reminded myself. I wasn't the cause of all the bad in my world. Despite having been told that, often, since becoming a teenager. I had not understood the magic that flowed deep within my veins. From the bully of ex-boyfriend to casual acquaintances along the way, I believed, I was to blame for every bad occurrence. No more. My magic did 'go-haywire' causing power outages, items to break, storms to flash across the sky. Only because I didn't know. I hadn't been taught. I didn't believe in me.

With my hands once again hovering above the crystal ball I peered into the cloudy crystal. Blurry shapes moved around in front of me. I squinted. As the image became clearer, I recognised the building next to the switchboard. The three men who now used the building as their office, weren't alone. As I moved my hands to wipe my eyes the image faded to nothing.

I felt myself sink into the nearest chair with a gentle thud. Sprinkles and Cinnamon flanked either side, checking I was okay. "I'm tired, but I'll be fine," I reassured them as an overwhelming exhaustion washed over me.

After a few deep breaths I felt much better. "How about a cup of tea?" I spoke aloud, finding strength in speaking into the space. Something I'd started years ago, along with my positive mantras, it helped allay my anxieties. The water in the kettle bubbled and hissed away. With my peppermint tea in my large purple mug, I returned to the table. Home. I let the feeling settle into my spirit, into my soul.

A knock at the door roused me from my daydream. How long I'd sat in contemplation I wasn't sure. Sprinkles yapped excitedly as he ran to the door, jumping up in an effort to open it. Cinnamon watched the commotion from her cozy pink cushion.

"Huge apologies for being late," Ned stood on the step, holding a tray with four brightly coloured cupcakes. "I thought I'd contribute dessert," he offered the tray to me.

"They're perfect!" I smiled, accepting the tray. Ned followed me into the kitchen. If he noticed the new additions on the table, he didn't comment.

"A light dinner, meats, cheeses, salads, and crackers. Have a seat, it won't take long for me to get ready." I removed the items from the fridge and cupboard, placing them on a wooden serving board on the table. Cutlery, plates, glasses and a bottle of apple juice and we were ready to eat. "Presents from my grandmother," I replied to Ned's unasked question, noting he kept giving the cauldron and the crystal ball sideways glances. "Yes, they work, linked to my magic, which I'm trying to get used to."

Ned picked a selection of meats, cheese and crackers. "Nothing surprises me in this town. My parents moved here many years ago. Most of my childhood was spent here. My parents and I have no magic to speak of. I've learnt though, that there are many ways to approach events and opportunities. I've developed a keen sense of whether a person is honest or untruthful. I can tell their intent. Don't ask me how. Sometimes I think the village itself has gifted me these skills, so I can help keep residents safe. Is that bonkers?"

I gazed into my friends deep brown eyes. "I think it's entirely possible, probable even." I picked at the food on my plate. The butterflies in my stomach were making too much ruckus for me to eat. Most likely my proximity to the handsome policeman. "You said you needed my help with something?"

Ned nodded. "I do. I assume you heard, saw or sensed that explosion earlier today?"

This time it was my turn to nod. I sipped my apple juice, enjoying the coolness of the drink.

"The cause of the explosion is a mystery. Sophie and I haven't found the site of the incident. We're sure the cause is magic in origin." Ned sipped his apple juice. "Would you be willing to use your intuition and help us work it out?"

I picked at the cheese and crackers on my plate. "Of course! I've been trying to figure it out, using my brain, but all I came up with was Brad. My instinct tells me it wasn't his magic." I paused, hoping a vision would flash in front of me and help solve the puzzle. "It's either someone playing with magic, or the Hartlys trying to attract interest in the village." I shrugged, unsure whether I was guessing or using my powers. "I will let you know when my intuition kicks in, or maybe my new toy will help us solve the mystery." I indicated the crystal ball.

"Thanks, I'd appreciate it." I melted at Ned's smile. The tingling in my body made me feel warm and gooey, in a good way. "Now, did I hear you say you have ice cream to go with the yummy cupcakes?"

The berry swirl ice cream complimented the cupcakes perfectly. "Thanks so much for the cupcakes," I said an hour later as we walked towards the door.

"Thank you for dinner. Sorry to leave so early, but I promised Sophie I'd relieve her so she could have a break," he responded, touching my arm. A shot of energy flew around my body. Looking into Ned's eyes I knew he felt it too.

Chapter Nineteen

Showered, dressed and with the animals fed by 6am, I turned on the television with trepidation. I breathed a sigh of relief as I didn't see Barbie's face on the screen. "Okay guys, it's another long day. I'll see you later this afternoon." Bert chirped goodbye, Cinnamon eyed me from my comfy chair. Sprinkles followed me to the door, his tail wagging hopefully.

I brushed my fingers along my lavender and rosemary on my way down the path. There was no sign of Margo in her garden. In my head I ran through the idea I wanted to bring up with Hazel.

"Inviting members of the founding families to join the council, or sit on a committee, to be involved in some of the decisions that directly impact on the residents of the village." Hazel repeated my suggestion back to me. She sipped her chai tea as she stared into the space over my head. From our table at the back of the café, Hazel could see customers coming and going. "I'm impressed. I should've thought of it myself. Especially after our discussion yesterday. Back before...before you were born...we had a committee that served as you suggest. Over the years Florence did away with it. Slowly eroding the openness, until she made all the decisions for the town."

Jess arrived at our table with two plates of food. One had a couple of toasted sandwiches, the other a selection of cupcakes. "Sorry it took so long," she said breathlessly. "It's been busy this morning already.

There are so many tourists coming to check out our town, which is always good for business." Jess's blonde hair was tied in a high ponytail, with a glittery gold ribbon wrapped around it. Her apron made of a matching glittery material, a stark contrast to her black leggings and t-shirt. Her magical helpers had been busy in the café overnight. The gold and silver streamers hung in delicate loops and chains around the walls. Midsummer Moonlight Masquerade posters hung on the walls. Floating above us, fairy lights blinked on and off in a criss-cross pattern.

"Thanks for the food and drink, don't worry about the delay, I was admiring the decorations, and enjoying the chance to sit and chat to Hazel." I ignored my rumbling stomach as I smiled at Jess.

"Rosie and Jazz came by yesterday afternoon with the decorations, to promote the ball. They thought it'd give people something positive to focus on, rather than the kerfuffle with the council and the business proposals." Jess smiled apologetically at Hazel, "No offence intended."

"None taken my dear. I think focusing on something positive and fun for the village is a brilliant idea," my grandmother reassured the café owner.

As Jess hurried back to attend to her customers, Hazel turned to me. "You were about to tell me something else?" If I wasn't getting used to it, her stare would have unnerved me.

I sipped my chai latte. The sugary cinnamon taste, infused with other herbs provided the energy boost I needed. "After Ned left, I couldn't sleep. I wrote down my idea, like a project plan. I researched the founding families and have listed those individuals I think would be assets to the council, but also who'd probably agree to join. I'm happy to contact them and ask them to come along to a meeting. After our morning meeting." I watched my grandmothers face for a clue to what she thought of my idea. "There's more," I added before giving her a chance to speak. "Maz invited me to a coven meeting at two this afternoon. I'd like to go if possible. Also, Ned has asked me to help investigate that explosion last night." As I stopped speaking, I watched Hazel.

She drank deeply from her chair latte. Then she picked up a toasted sandwich, motioning for me to do the same. Only after I had my mouth full of food, did she speak.

"Your idea is right on track. We'll run it by the existing members. I imagine they would jump at the chance to have more people on board, especially with the goings on in the village. Why don't you contact the founding families, after the meeting, and invite them to a meeting tonight, at 6pm. We want to make sure we leave it open for any of the founding families who want to, the opportunity to join us on council. We'll have measures in place to ensure their honesty and intent. That should leave you enough time to meet Maz and the others." She glanced at the watch on her wrist. "We've still a couple of hours before our morning meeting. Let me tell you about what I learnt last night, and what I think caused the explosion."

"Ah yes, your time with Leopold, and Mikal." I said as Hazel picked up a second toasted sandwich. "The explosion didn't feel like someone's magic going wrong, or something that the Hartlys would have concocted. They want people to come to the village, not be scared away by ominous explosions."

I gazed around the room as Hazel finished eating. There were more customers than normal. As I tuned into their conversations, I caught the words *quaint, cute, mystical,* and *magical.* Misty Vale's regular tourists tended to be grey nomads, or people who'd heard about our unusual crafts and arts. Intuition told me most of the customers were curious and bore no ill will to the town.

"An increase in tourism, or even new residents is good for the village," Hazel agreed, reading my mind. "As long as they don't want to build monstrous, gaudy tourist attractions. Joining our weekly markets as stallholders, buying our bespoke culinary and crafty goodies, or signing up for our workshops are acceptable options." Hazel returned her sandwich to her plate. "My time with Leopold was productive. He confirmed that neither Robbie, or the Hartlys can sue us or the council for refusing an application. There are written rules and laws built into the fabric of our village that prevents such actions. The council can evoke an old law to force them to leave town, but as a last resort only. The repercussions of doing so would be felt throughout the village for generations." Hazel's face looked so serious, I didn't ask her for further explanation. "On a more positive note, Mikal can build a programme that provides the council, us, and the police a range of useful technological tools. He's going to demonstrate his software programme later in the week." My grandmother paused as she finished her chai. "The explosion was the result of a resident, or a group of people, trying to layer a protection spell around the perimeter of the village. There's a place on the edge of the woodland near one of the roads into town where you can see the remnants. I could show you, but I want you to trust your intuition. Take my jeep. Find the place and see if you can deduce who may have been trying to protect our town. Make sure you are back by 8:45am. I'll print off copies of your plan for our meeting this morning." Grandma stood, leaving no room for discussion. "I'll take one cupcake, you take the other, please don't spill crumbs in the jeep."

I thought she was joking, but in case she was serious, I tucked the cupcake into a napkin and placed it in my bag. "Thank you, Grandma. I'll be back in plenty of time for the meeting." I waved at Jess as I left the café and hopped into the driver's seat of the jeep. I'd wondered why Hazel had parked out the front of the café, instead of at the back of the council building. She'd planned my expedition all along.

With no thought except the cause of the explosion, and the road rules, I drove to the main road in and out of Misty Vale. In place of a rigid t-intersection, the road that brought visitors to Misty Vale was windy. Little more than a dirt track in places, widening out into a two-lane road in others, it was a bumpy ride. A well-worn track. The sign at the town limits welcomed visitors. Behind the town marker, the native woodland came into its own. I drove the jeep along a side road, trusting my intuition to lead me. In the clearing I noted evidence of a campfire.

Eyeing my black flat shoes doubtfully, I stepped my way carefully along a dirt path. At least it felt like a path. Tapping into my intuition I sensed the leftover aura of those who'd walked this way less than twenty-four hours ago. The smell of a fire wafted past. An old fire, a small one, as part of a spell to protect the village. As if I were staring through my crystal ball, I saw an image a few metres in front of me. A hazy image, of four people. I couldn't make out their words, though I watched their actions. After holding hands and chanting they each threw a handful of dust onto the fire. The ground wobbled as in the image the explosion shook the area. The image disappeared, leaving me alone in a clearing filled with magical residue. I took my phone out of my pocket and messaged Ned –

I found the site of the explosion, near the rest area on the road out of town. I'll stay here for half an hour.

I headed back to my car to wait for the policeman. Scribbling down as many details on the image as I could remember, I filled a couple of pages of my notebook. As I checked my watch for the third time, the police car drove into the clearing. Sophie and Ned climbed out of the white sedan.

I jumped out of my car to greet them. "Now, bear in mind I found it by following my magic intuition," I started, "And while I was here, I saw an image, of what happened last night. A group of four people that I couldn't identify, were casting a spell to protect the town from…unscrupulous people. They threw something that looked like dust, into a small fire, and caused the explosion." I led the police to the scene of the fire as I spoke.

Sophie pulled her tablet out of the pocket of her vest. "You couldn't see who they were?"

I shook my head. "The image was blurry, like in the olden days when we had to tune televisions into the station." I thought back to the image. "My sense is they are youngish, maybe our age, and female, at least two of them." I used my other senses to piece it together. "Maybe from one of the founding families, though I can't be sure. There's no lasting damage, apart from this haze of magic, which will likely dissipate over the next day or so."

Ned made some notes in his notebook, as Sophie took photos with the tablet. "How do you know that?" The admiration in his voice surprised me.

"I'm not sure, my intuition, or my magic, whatever you call it, is growing stronger," I tried to shrug it off, not keen to mention my crystal ball in front of Sophie. She was lovely, and young, but not from Misty Vale. "I'm sorry I can't figure out any more details."

"You have helped, because if you're sure this isn't a crime, we won't need to waste time and effort looking into it," Ned reasoned. "If you do think of anything else, please let us know." Ned fell into step beside me as we returned to our cars. His fingers brushed against mine, sending tingles throughout my body.

"Over here," Sophie called us to a pile of leaves and twigs. Lying across the top of one of the twigs was a silver chain with a blue crystal pendant. She picked up the item using a clear plastic bag she pulled out of her pocket. "Do you recognise it?"

I thought back to last time I saw Maz. None of the woman wore a necklace with a blue stone, did they? "I don't think so. The crystal is a lapis lazuli, though I'm not exactly sure why I know that." I ran my eyes over the area where Sophie found the necklace. Nothing else stood out as part of the previous evening's enchantment. A tiny red velvet pouch popped into my mind, but I couldn't see anything like it on the ground. I turned to face Ned. "I've got a meeting at 9am, so if you don't need me anymore, I'll head off. If I think of anything else, I'll let you know straight away."

Ned checked his watch. "It's nearly 8:45am. We'll let you know if we have any more questions." I could tell by his face, that Ned wanted to say something else. He glanced at Sophie.

"Oh, before I forget, Hazel and I may be hosting a town meeting tonight. I can give you more information after we talk to the other councillors," I added, as I climbed back into the jeep's driver's seat.

My watch told me it was exactly 8:45am as I walked through the back door near our office. Hazel wasn't there, so I headed straight for the meeting room. "Did you set all this up?" I asked, taking in the table set with copies of my plan, cakes, mugs, plates, coffee and tea bags.

"I only got the paperwork organised; Sharon is responsible for the food and drink." Hazel replied, as she added a notebook and pen to one of the piles of papers positioned around the table. "I've written out some information on each of the main families. I know you've done your research, but what I know may come in handy."

Before I could answer, Sharon, Steve, and Joan arrived. "There's hot water in the kettle if anyone wants a cuppa," Sharon placed the kettle on the runner in the centre of the table.

Joan passed the plate of mini chocolate cakes around as Sharon filled each mug with water. "Thank you all for returning today," Hazel began to speak as people settled into their chairs. "I'm guessing you saw the circus set up next door. They chose that vacant building on purpose, to irritate us. They could have easily used one of the other buildings they own." Hazel crossed her arms. Immediately uncrossing them again she leant forward. "Jane came up with an idea to give us strength in numbers. She suggested we invite members of the families that founded Misty Vale to take an active role in the council. Like we used to, before I ran away and Florence took control."

I looked over the top of my cup at the three council members. I smiled at each of them as I shared my plans for the meeting that evening.

"I think that is a great idea," Sharon spoke first. "I've got a lot of their email addresses, and telephone numbers. We keep in touch. A lot of the families aren't happy with Brad's plans. I think if we invite them all to come along tonight and explain our plans, and see who's interested, we'll have a full council by the end of the week."

Steve and Joan nodded their agreement.

As Hazel chatted to the others, I sent emails off to representatives of the families, using the addresses Sharon provided. I explained who I was, and why we were hosting the meeting. Within ten minutes of sending the email, I'd received twelve emails from residents confirming attendance. "We've received twelve acceptances to the meeting tonight," I told the group as Joan piled up our used plates. I neglected to tell them about the emails from Brad, David and Robbie, sitting unread in our inbox.

Chapter Twenty

I knocked on Maz's door with minutes to spare. The second time in twenty-four hours that I barely made an appointment on time. Did an awakening of magic make time move differently? "Jane, I'm so glad you could make it," Maz opened the door and led me to her living area, where Jazz, Rosie, and Shaz were already seated. Was it odd that none of the four women were on the list of the descendants I'd emailed earlier? I knew many of the founding families chose to change their names, when my parents' left town, to bring me up, away from magic. Marrying another spirit element had been taboo back then. Now residents were free to marry whomever they wanted to – magic or non-magic.

As soon as I took my seat, I knew I was with the women who'd attempted to cast the protection enchantment. I decided to keep that knowledge to myself for now. "Sorry I'm late, Hazel and I are organising a town meeting tonight. Anyone from the founding families who are interested in joining council are welcome to attend." I said conversationally, hoping for a clue as to their motives, and whether they belonged to the original Misty Vale families.

The four women exchanged a glance I couldn't quite fathom. I decided to let the matter lie, for now. "I loved the decorations at the café," I beamed. "How many days until the Midsummer Moonlight Masquerade?"

Shaz clapped her hands together. "Eight days," she exclaimed excitedly. "That's why we called this extraordinary meeting. We wanted to work on the plans and thought you might like to help."

"We also wanted to ask you a question," Rosie spoke quietly as she passed me a plate of daintily cut shortbread stars.

I picked up a cookie covered with pale pink icing and pink sprinkles. "Ask away. Hmm, delicious," I added as the biscuit crumbled in my mouth.

Jazz leant towards me. Instinctively I moved back a fraction, hoping she didn't notice. My internal radar suggested caution. "Where do you stand on the business applications? I know you sided with Hazel and the council, but is it your personal view that Brad's plans are wrong for the village, or would you be open to learning more about and supporting the exciting new business opportunities?"

"I didn't see that coming at all." I told Hazel as I recounted the story an hour later. "I agreed to help with the set up for the ball. I muttered something about business opportunities in the best interest of the village are always welcome and pretended I received a message from you and had to leave."

Hazel nodded. "I feared the Brad's offer of growing businesses and incentives for the village would generate support. Have you received more interest from your email?"

"Yes, in addition to the names I sent you before, I've heard from half a dozen interested parties. I'm surprised that none of four women on the committee are listed as members of the founding families."

Hazel stood and motioned for me to follow her. I hardly recognised the room I'd identified as the place to hold this evening's meeting. "How did you get time to do all this?" I asked in awe. There were fifty chairs set up, and a table with an urn, cups, plates, a barrel of biscuits, and napkins. Around the walls hundreds of little white fairy lights flickered.

Hazel held her hands out, the palms of her hands upwards. "I figured I was out of practice. I needed to see if I could still do it."

"I'm impressed," I told my grandmother. "I'd not thought of using magic for things like that."

"Generally, I don't, but there are exceptions to every rule. It's been a big day, and we've got about an hour before we have to be back here. Let me buy you a snack or something a little healthier than a cupcake." Hazel gently touched my back, propelling me out of the room.

"A sensible idea," I agreed as we exited the building.

I groaned. "We should've headed out the back door," I muttered to my grandmother. Roberto's voice echoed through the front room of the building, and into the street as we walked past. I saw Barbie, Nicholas, and the Hartly brothers. "I don't want to know what they're saying..." I stopped as I heard a voice, I thought I recognised. I put my fingers to my lips. Hazel nodded. We stopped walking as I pretended to rummage in my bag looking for something. I strained my ears, trying to pick where I knew the voice from. Eventually I picked my notebook out of my bag. "Here it is," I exclaimed more loudly than I had to. "Thank goodness I didn't leave it behind." Hazel and I walked on to the café.

After ordering a vegetarian pizza and ginger beer we sat at the booth we liked, at the back of the café. Buzzing with customers, Jess and her helpers were busy. "Wednesday night is pizza night," Jess said a little breathlessly. "Luckily I buy in bulk, or we would have run out by now." She handed me a jug of ginger beer and two glasses.

I chose the table as far away from the door as possible.

"Your powers are getting stronger," Hazel observed. "You're noticing words and actions, and sensing auras and magic from times past. The ability to pick up on residue and see images isn't a skill we all have," Grandma acknowledged, patting my hand reassuringly.

I was surprised at her statement. "You can, can't you?"

"I used to be able to. I haven't tried for ages. I can with you, my only living relative. I was never an investigator, nor am I as inquisitive as you are."

One of Jess's helpers, a teen with a fairylike face, fair skin, blonde hair and small ears, arrived at our table with our pizza. "My name is Fleur. If you need anything else, please let me know." She gave a little bow as she left our table.

"My intuition is telling me we need to eat and get back to the room. Though it may be nerves, or the nerve of Roberto, that has me a little on edge." I picked up a slice of pizza. I saw capsicum, onion, mushrooms, broccoli, zucchini, and cheese, and the flavour didn't disappoint.

Hazel raised her eyebrows. "Between the two of us we will be able to assess the intent of the attendees. Leopold confirmed we have the right to refuse nominations from anyone who's working with Robbie and the Hartlys or intends to benefit from their businesses. I've infused a truth enchantment in the council application forms. It won't be evident to them, but we'll know of their intent when we review the forms."

I put the slice of pizza down in amazement. "That's a terrific idea. Maybe I'm overreacting. I thought I recognised a female voice earlier. Not the reporter or Florence's daughters. My imagination is in overdrive, with everything that's going on."

Hazel patted my arm sympathetically. "It's a lot, but we'll get through it. Life in Misty Vale isn't normally so intense."

Cathy from The Crafty Owl came into the café. She spotted us and ran up to our table. "Hazel, Jane, you'd better get back to the council building. An alarm is going off at the back of the building. I was heading to my car when I heard it. I tried to see what was going on, but there was a weird fog swirling around. Magic still scares me a little. Which is silly seeing as I've lived here a couple of years."

Hazel and I jumped up and waved our thanks to Jess and her helpers as we raced out the door. "Thank you, Cathy. Do you need one of us to come with you to your car?" I asked as we headed to the carpark.

"I'm all good, thank you, for asking. Good luck." Cathy walked briskly in the opposite direction as we marched directly into the fog.

It was dense, sticky, and a weird bluey red colour. Not purple, more a brown, murky muck. "Have you seen anything like this before?" I asked Hazel as we stepped deeper into the fog, in the direction of the back entrance to the old switchboard building.

"Not for a long time," she replied. Her voice sounded odd, as the fog's tendrils got in my ears and up my nose. "We need to pull a coat of protection around us," she called firmly.

My eyes squeezed shut tightly as a bright light flashed in front of me. I opened them immediately. "Are you okay?" I asked into the fog as I called my deep purple velvet cloak of protection towards me. I'd been calling on my cloak for years, as a way to ease my anxiety. Not for a second did I think it was a magic spell.

A warm hand reached for mine. "Yes, I'm fine now. Grab my hand so we don't get separated. That's what this fog does. Whoever cast it wants to disorient us. To cause us, and anyone who comes along to the meeting to get lost in the mist forever. An air element working with a water element if I'm not mistaken. Can you see the star?"

I looked up and was surprised to see a green neon star flashing a few metres in front of us. "Yes, I can."

"Keep walking towards that star. Keep hold of my hand. Visualise an easy, clear path through the mist. Don't get distracted."

"I wish you hadn't said that last part," I groaned. "It's like telling me not to think of oranges."

"Focus Clara!" My grandmothers tone left no room for anything but focusing on the star, the path, her hand and a way through the fog.

I pressed my feet down firmly, with each step. I pictured paving stones under my feet, odd shaped, oblong, smooth rocks, the type that were common around riverbeds. The glow from the star got brighter and brighter. After what seemed like hours, my grandmother's profile came into view. "Can you hear that?" I asked. A strange sound whispering around me, grew louder the closer I got to the star.

"Shh, keep moving." Hazel tugged my hand, dragging me the last few metres. She yanked open the back door, and we tumbled into the building. The door slammed shut behind us.

"Who was whispering out there?" I asked shakily, still a little rattled by the fog.

"Lost souls. Those who stepped into the mist years ago and never found their way out." Hazel sounded wobbly.

"Have we lost any residents to the fog tonight?" I asked, worried I'd caused harm to innocents by inviting them along to a meeting where a sinister mist surrounded the venue.

"I'm not sure." She held out both her hands. "Grab my hands and picture the fog disintegrating. Visualise it getting lighter and lighter until it disappears all together. If you see anyone wandering in the fog wearing modern day clothes, set them to one side first. My instructions will make sense when we start. Right, are you ready? Start now."

Holding Hazel's hands tightly, with my eyes shut, I found a couple of people wandering in the fog. I led them to safety. Then when I couldn't find any others, I concentrated on getting rid of the fog. My skin tingled, my hands stung. I didn't let go until I couldn't see any fog particles left anywhere. Slowly I opened my eyes. As they adjusted to my surroundings, I noticed my grandmother's face was pale. As I loosened my grip on her hands she fell backwards. "Grandma," I called as I caught her, and helped her to the closest chair. "Here, drink this," I retrieved a half empty water bottle from my handbag.

Hazel drank a little and moved so she sat a little straighter in the chair. "I'll be okay. No need to make a fuss."

Not taking my eyes from her face, I pulled out my mobile, only moving my eyes to punch out a message to Ned. Crouched in front of

Hazel I didn't move until someone banged on the door five minutes later.

"I'm perfectly fine," Hazel said as Ned, Sophie and a young man in a paramedic uniform walking into the corridor.

"Of course you are Hazel, but as I've asked young Jack here to check you over, please oblige him and let him do his job," Ned said in his best charming voice. "I need to talk to Jane, but Sophie will be right here with you," he added.

I let Ned steer me away, into the room we'd set up for the evenings get together. I heard Jack and Sophie talking to Hazel. I exhaled, not realising I'd been holding my breath. "Thank you for coming so quickly."

"We'd received several calls about the fog and were on our way to assess the threat level. There's no fog left out there. Do you know who caused it, and why? And are you okay? I think Jack should check you as well. That could have been a toxic mist. I mean we've seen weirder things here." Ned looked stricken at the thought something could have happened to me.

Without over thinking it, I turned and hugged the handsome policeman. Not a polite it's nice to see you hug. More a thank goodness you are here, and I like you very much hug. After the initial surprise, Ned hugged me back.

Ned eventually broke the embrace. "What happened here?" I turned to focus on the large room Hazel had set up so beautifully. Chairs were knocked over, water from the urn was lying in a pool on the floor, the coffee and tea bags thrown on the floor. "It's like a mini tornado came through here."

"It is, isn't it," I muttered. "An air elemental. The Hartly's must have at least a couple of locals working with them.

"I take it that it wasn't you who cancelled the meeting tonight?" Ned asked as he started tipping the chairs back up.

"It wasn't me, but I can guess who it was. I'll fix these up later." I took Ned's hand and led him out of the room, shutting the door behind us. "Sophie, can you sit with Hazel for a few more minutes? Grandma, please rest, I'll be right back."

Ned still held my hand as I left the building. "Are you sure you should do this?" he asked.

"No, but they can't get away with this," I replied as I marched into the open door of the building next door. "Roberto, we need to talk. This is not your town, or yours Brad, or David. You can't conjure thick fogs, or ransack a meeting room, or cancel a council meeting, because you don't like what might happen."

"Jane," Roberto sneered. "Was it you playing around with magic? I hear there was a problem with a fog. And were you planning a meeting tonight? It's such a shame, it appears no one has turned up. You surely can't think the Hartlys, or I had anything to do with it. I don't possess magic, and the Hartlys are pillars of this community. I'm happy to arrange a meeting to discuss a way forward, where we all get want we want."

Luckily for Roberto that Ned held my hand tightly. That, and a deep-seated instinct not to lose my temper here, in front of these people. I had to remain in control. I stood tall, looked Roberto in the eye, aware that others were crowding around to listen. The reporter, members of the community. Now wasn't the time or place to lose it. I gave Roberto what I hoped was a withering stare, swung around and walked back out of the building. Sniggering, and words I refused to listen to, echoed around me as I returned to see how my grandmother was feeling.

"Thank you," I whispered to Ned as we approached Grandma and the others. Reluctantly, we released our fingers.

"Hazel will be okay, once she has a strong cup of tea, some food, and a good night's sleep." Jack patted Hazel on her shoulder.

"I'm right here young man," Hazel's voice reminded me of a school-teacher admonishing her pupil. Her voice softened as she continued, "Thank you, for making sure I'm not suffering any ill-effects of that mist. I do appreciate it, but I value my independence."

"Yes, thank you Jack, Sophie, Ned," I echoed. I turned to Hazel. "I'll drive you home and walk to my place. We can reconvene tomorrow and work out our next steps." I locked the building as the five of us exited.

"Do you know who started the fog?" Ned asked quietly as Sophie helped Hazel into the jeep's passenger seat.

"I've a couple of ideas. I don't think they meant to hurt anyone. Though I do think Roberto put them up to it, and he wouldn't care if anyone got hurt," I responded, some of my earlier anger returning.

"I'll try and call around later if that's okay, but it might be tomorrow morning before I get a chance." Ned sounded worn as he held my door open.

My fingers held his arm briefly, sending tingles around my body as our skin touched. "I imagine you'll be kept busy with call outs. We'll be fine, and I'll make you a cuppa whenever you can make it. You and Sophie take care out there." We all waved as I started the jeep, leaving the police behind to respond to concerned residents.

"I am quite all right you know," my grandmother said for the tenth time as I made her a cuppa and a couple of pieces of toast. "You need to get home to your pets, have some food and a sleep yourself. Unless Ned is coming around, in which case you still need to get home."

I blushed. If she was teasing me, she must be feeling more like herself.

"Go on, I'll be fine. We'll meet tomorrow morning. I'll pick you up and we'll work out a way forward. A good night's sleep is what we need." Hazel crouched to pat Esmeralda who'd finally come out of her bed to check on her human.

I tried for my sternest voice, "You tuck yourself into bed, and if you feel sick at all, you let me know or ring an ambulance. Who knows what toxic gunk was swirling around in that fog."

Hazel frowned. She looked me up and down, and chuckled. "You might like to work on your bossy voice."

My pets were happy to see me. Sprinkles and Cinnamon met me at the door. Bert chirped good naturedly as I entered the kitchen. "Hi guys, what a crazy day," I told my family. "I'm here now let's get you guys fed." Bert's seed was first. My hand shook a little, but I managed to get most of it into his feed bowl. Cinnamon's dry cat food came next. She lived here before all of us, so she had first dibs. Sprinkles had learnt to wait for his food. He ran in circles around the table while Cinnamon ate. When I finally put the dog bowl with his food in it on the floor, he raced around my legs and hoovered the food as if he'd not eaten for days.

As my pets ate and settled into their evening routine, I eyed my comfy armchair. "I'd love to snuggle in there with a book, some berries, chocolate and a glass of fizzy water," I told Sprinkles as stood in front of me, wagging his tail. "But there's no way I can sit still after the events of the day." I rummaged in the fridge and came up with a plate of food. A few strawberries, a chocolate bar, leftover cheese and crackers, and some grapes. I poured a large glass of water from the tap. Armed with my supplies I sat at the kitchen table and opened my laptop.

On a blank word document, I noted down the issues – Robbie and the Hartly brothers, whether I trusted the new friends I'd made, how to host a town meeting, or was it even worth it...I deleted the page and opted for my notebook and pen. I scribbled the same questions down and stared at the page, willing an answer to jump out.

My eyes wandered to the magical tools sitting on my table. I found a fresh candle and placed it my cauldron. Taking out the old candle and sprigs of herbs I sprinkled some dried herbs and cinnamon pieces into the pot. With my fingers touching the cold cast iron I willed the candle to light. As I watched, the candle flame hissed to life. The metal warmed under my touch. The aromas of the dried herbs permeated the air.

Turning to the crystal ball I touched the stone. Cold under my fingers, as I held my hands on the object, the crystal slowly warmed to my touch. The imperfections in the stone zigzagged, like a fuzzy out of tune television. I blinked my eyes a couple of times. It didn't help much. *Try tuning it in* a voice whispered. Tune it in? Ah maybe, I moved my hands to the left, right, up, and down as if I was tuning it. Slowly the image came into focus.

The first picture showed me Maz, Shaz, Jazz, and Rosie trying to set the protection spell around the village. From my vantage point as bystander, I noticed that while Maz and Shaz were concentrating on the enchantment, Jazz and Rosie sprinkled something into the fire, from a small dark blue box. "Did they booby trap the spell?" I asked aloud, startling Sprinkles who'd finally decided to lie on his cushion. The female voice earlier, talking to Roberto, could have been Jazz. Instinct told me that Jazz and Rosie were working with Roberto. I'd still to figure out why.

The next scene was of the fog at the back of the building. I recognised some of the members of the founding families as they hopped out of their vehicles to attend the meeting. Two young women walked up to each person, spoke to them, turning them away. Even through the fog I recognised Cindy and Mindy Hartly. Why would founding family members interested in joining the council listen to Florence's daughters? They couldn't all be wanting to grow their businesses or align with the Hartlys.

The crystal zapped, like it was about to show me a third image, but then the screen went blank. I moved my hands around the ball to not avail. Maybe it needed to re-charge. I know I did, but I didn't expect I'd sleep much.

I flipped through my notebook until I found the page with the names of the families, their magical abilities and their allegiances. "It doesn't help that some residents changed their surnames," I told Cinnamon. She was sitting at my feet looking at me. "All the elementals – fire, air, water, earth, and spirit. Is there a way to know who's who? And who is working for Roberto, or Brad?" Cinnamon nudged my leg. I picked her up, positioning her on my lap. "How do I know who to trust? Apart from Ned and Hazel?" My familiar headbutted the hand where I wore my ring. She did the same with my necklace.

"Of course! Thank you." I kissed the top of my cat's head. As I made to place her back on the floor, she jumped agily on the table, swotted the metal box with her paw, before daintily alighting.

I rearranged the items on the table, so the box sat in front of me. As I opened it, I noticed a couple of indentations I'd not noticed before. My ring, which I could not remove from my finger, since slipping it on a month ago, slid easily along my finger, landing in the ring-shaped spot in the box. I unclasped my necklace; the stones sat neatly in their spot next to my ring.

With a loud *zap, zing, zap* all the stones lit up, as if I'd plugged them into an electric socket. I averted my eyes from the intense light. The crystal ball slowly illuminated. The smoky haze in the divination tool slowly cleared. In front of me, a scene played out. A room full of people.

I recognised Hazel, Florence Hartly, her daughters, and her brothers in law. Next to Hazel were some figures I couldn't make out. I recognised some of the faces, but I didn't know them by name.

I needed information on the founding families, those with elemental magic. Devlin, Murphy, Eliott, Wilson, Thorne, Dean, Sparks, Gale, names associated with the elements. My eyelids drooped, as I tried to focus on my intuition, rather than my brain. I was trying too hard to figure out the missing piece of the puzzle. I turned away from the new magic tools and started up my laptop.

An hour later I yawned. Using my investigative skills, I'm managed to find the information I'd been searching for. "Maz isn't directly related to Florence. That's a relief." The sick feeling in my stomach eased a little. "But she's part of the Murphy family." My pup looked up with interest as I voiced my thoughts. "Shaz is a Dean, Marigold's niece." Sprinkles wandered over with his ball. I took it gently from his mouth and rolled it across the floor. He scampered after it, taking it back to his cushion to gnaw at it. Marigold wasn't all bad. Sure, she started a fire in a warehouse, but Florence had been behind that.

Rosie and Jazz were different, neither grew up in Misty Vale. Their parents were previous inhabitants of the village. Not Wilsons, Elliots, Deans, Murphys or Devlins. Jazz's mother was a Hartly, cousin to Brad and David. Rosie was the only one I couldn't trace. Even with her parents' names an internet search didn't provide additional information.

I yawned again. The digital clock on my laptop advised me it was nearly midnight. "I doubt I'll be able to sleep, but I know you'd like to be able to," I cooed to Bert as I turned out the kitchen light. Sprinkles and Cinnamon watched as I headed for the bedroom. Once it became clear I was actually climbing into bed, both animals jumped up to keep me company.

Chapter Twenty-One

I sat up in a panic. My pillow was across the floor; the blankets kicked down to the bottom of my bed. My pets looked at me from the doorway. Gradually my heart rate slowed to a more acceptable level. I inhaled and exhaled deeply. What had woken me? I must have been in a deep dreamless sleep. At least I didn't remember my dream. Nothing else in the room looked out of place.

Maybe I'd had a nightmare after all. It'd account for the dishevelled blankets. On my way to the kitchen, I checked the rest of my cottage. Nothing appeared out of place. My mobile told me it was only 5am. I checked for messages, thinking Ned might have texted me. Nothing. I sighed. I was being silly. Ned probably got caught up with work. I hoped that didn't mean there'd been any other incidents since the weird fog the previous evening.

Leaving my animals to their food, I headed for the shower. A long hot shower to wash away negative vibes. I wiggled my fingers and toes, deliberately letting go of anxiety, angst, pain, I rubbed my hands under the water, clearing away any residual energy. A clean slate, a new day. A positive start.

I'd almost finished dressing when I heard a knock at front door. "It was after 10pm by the time I finished my paperwork. I thought that was too late to call in." Ned handed me a tray with a tall takeaway cup and a caramel nut muffin on it. "I hope this begins to make up for that." The lanky handsome policeman grinned, as I finished pulling on my sock.

"When you bring breakfast, of course all is forgiven. Although you've done nothing to be forgiven for." I smiled at him. "Come in, if you've got time."

"I'd love to, but I'm due back at the station. There were some odd incidents overnight. I'd like to discuss them with you and Hazel, if you are free later this morning," he added hopefully, his voice tilting a little at the end of the sentence.

"We'll make time for you Ned. I must say I'm intrigued. Can you give me any details now?" I sipped the takeaway coffee, enjoying the bittersweet flavoured caramel latte.

Ned pulled his notebook from his jacket pocket. He ran his finger down one of the pages. "Strange noises, weird lights, lightening, isolated storms, some locals reported an earthquake, others swore a mini tornedo moved through their house. We received more than a dozen different calls. We're following up on each one this morning."

An image of Roberto conducting an orchestra of elementals flashed in front of my eyes. I clenched my feet to steady myself. "Robbie, and the Hartlys coercing some of our residents to create havoc. If they cause enough mayhem and then come in and save the village from it, people will think they're wonderful." I suggested.

Ned grinned, "This is why we're going to come and talk to you, and Hazel. You think like an investigator, and you know the magic side."

"I'm quickly learning more about it, that's for sure," I agreed. "My intuition appears to be getting stronger, thank goodness." I put the coffee and muffin on the table and hugged Ned. It felt right, not awkward or inappropriate. "Thanks for coming around, and for breakfast. I'll let Hazel know we'll expect you later in the morning."

When we let go of each other, Ned kissed my forehead. "I just wish I could stay, but we've got to make sure the locals know Sophie and I are on top of the spate of...whatever this is. The last thing we need is Brad bringing in his own law enforcement, or threatening to, which would be just as bad."

I watched from the doorway as Ned returned to his car. As he drove away, I scanned the horizon. Tiny puffs of smoke appeared on the horizon. A couple were blue, others were pink.

"How nice of Ned," I told my animals as I sat to finish my early morning snack.

I'd almost finished my muffin and coffee when there was a knock on my door. "Hazel, you're looking much better this morning." I hugged my grandmother as she walked through the door.

"I feel a lot better, after a good night's sleep." She raised her eyebrows as she noticed the takeaway container. "Did you grab yourself some breakfast?"

I looked at my empty cup and laughed. "No, Ned dropped by with this for me. I could still go for a second breakfast, with you."

Hazel reached down and patted Cinnamon as my cat rubbed her back along my grandma's legs. Sprinkles sat back eyeing my grandmother, concerned Hazel's grumpy cat might be hiding behind her. "I think that's a great idea."

I checked my pets had enough water in their bowls. "You guys be good; I'll be home later this afternoon." I tickled Sprinkles under his chin, and stroked Cinnamon's back.

As we hopped into my grandmother's jeep a couple of bright streaks of lightning flashed across the sky. "Hmm," she said as she started the engine. "Smoke, lights, noises, we have a mystery to solve."

I clicked my seat belt in place. "Ned and Sophie are going to call in later today, to get our views on what's been going on. I'm pretty sure Robbie and the Hartly's are coercing locals to create havoc, so they can save us all from the magic gone haywire. Do you think we can figure out the details by lunchtime?"

The Milky Bar door swung open as I reached to open it. David Hartly nodded curtly at me as he pushed past us onto the footpath. He strode off quickly, clearly not keen on speaking to us. Hazel frowned at his back. "Manners never hurt anyone," she muttered at the broad-shouldered navy jacket.

Roberto and Brad Hartly were huddled together at one of the tables near the door. As Hazel and I lined up to place our order, I felt their eyes burning a hole in our backs. As I turned, undecided as to whether I'd speak to them, the door opened as they exited the café. "It'll be a much nicer breakfast now," Hazel commented.

"What can I get you ladies this morning?" Jess asked with her customary smile. Behind her one of her helpers was making coffees, another was popping breakfast items onto small blue plates.

"Let's have two large caramel lattes and a couple of cinnamon scrolls please Jess," I replied.

"Certainly. Are you eating in, or taking away?" Jess asked.

I looked at Hazel. I enjoyed eating in the café, but with the weird goings on, I would feel better talking at the office. "Let's get to work early. I want to make a dent on the paperwork," I suggested. Hazel nodded her agreement.

The door swung open. A scruffy man entered. In his late sixties, with a wild grey-white beard, and a cap pulled down tightly, he muttered to himself as we passed him. Hazel turned, her gaze following the newcomer.

"What's wrong? Do you recognise him?" I asked her.

"I think so, but I can't remember where I know him from," she shook her head. "Enough distractions, let's get this day happening."

We walked around the corner towards our office and nearly ran into Maz. "Jane! I'm so glad I ran into you. We've had to change the date of the Midsummer Moonlight Masquerade. Brad and Robbie have generously offered to their help so we can host the event this afternoon." She turned to Hazel. "They wanted me to ask you if it'd be possible to hold off on the town meeting until tomorrow. I know you're not happy with their plans, but this event is important to the village."

It was only after Maz finished speaking that I noticed Nicholas's camera set up in the doorway of the building. I glanced at Hazel. "I'm sure we could host the town meeting tomorrow. It will give us more time to invite interested residents. We've got some work this morning that we can't postpone. I'll come and find you when we're finished."

"That's fantastic Jane. We'll be at the showground. I'll see you there." Maz walked off before I could respond. I took Hazel's arm and ushered her into the relative safety of our office.

"I can't believe I misjudged Maz and the others," Hazel said with a huff.

"Don't feel bad, you weren't the only one," I said, opening my laptop. "I'm going to contact all those who responded initially, and reschedule the meeting for tomorrow morning," I said scrolling through my emails. "Not many of the locals who were supposed to attend last night have contacted us. What do you think about extending the invitation to all the villagers."

"Not a bad idea," Hazel conceded as her mobile beeped.

While she attended to her caller, I composed and sent the emails and created a post for social media.

"That was Beatrix from The Magic Cauldron. There's been an influx of people coming into the shop buying ingredients for spells and incantations. She thought we should know, with all the odd events happening around the village." Hazel said as she returned her mobile to her desk. "I'll investigate that, if you arrange tomorrow's meeting. How are you feeling about attending the masquerade ball...it is too much?"

I walked around the side of my grandmother's desk and patted her on the shoulder. "I've already emailed all the participants and posted on social media. I'll make sure the room is set first thing tomorrow morning. I'm not sure how I feel about the ball. I'll go, even though I don't really want to. It'll give me a chance to discover more about those four, whether they are all working with Brad. It'll be interesting to see who else may be working with them. I'll make sure I protect myself. Will you be okay here by yourself?"

Hazel looked me up and down and snorted. "Of course I will, but thanks for worrying about me. You be careful."

Chapter Twenty-Two

I almost didn't recognise the showground pavilion. The old wooden building had received a magic makeover. Tiny white fairy lights covered the externals surface of the white wooden building. The path from the carpark to the building was covered in red carpet, with a golden rope fence directing guests from their vehicles to the building. I walked up the steps and entered the building from the verandah into the large front room.

"Jane!" Shaz ran up to me, embracing me, as I stepped into the space.

The polished wooden floorboards sparkled with the fairy dust sprinkled on its surface. The walls were covered in a shimmering gold paint that sparkled under the lights of the hundreds of little fairy lights strung around the room. "I'm not sure what help you need, this looks amazing as it is," I replied to Shaz, wishing I didn't have to doubt my new friends.

Shaz tucked her arm into mine. "There's always something to do," she said. "We're so fortunate Robbie and Brad organised the caterers, and enough fancy dress and masks for the whole town."

"That's generous," I said begrudgingly. "Didn't the residents mind the change in date?" As soon as I had a chance, I'd message Ned and let him know where I was. As much as I'd love to be in his arms waltzing around the dance floor, I meant as a precaution, in case the event wasn't as innocent as it appeared to be.

"Oh no, not when Brad offered to refund double the price of their tickets to attend," Jazz said as she joined us.

I tried hard not to cringe. I didn't want my magic creating chaos in this beautiful venue. "What can I do to help?"

"Choose an outfit, and a mask. After you join us for a toast," Rosie said as she led us towards the side of the room where a side table was laden with champagne flutes.

"Passionflower juice," Maz added. "Non-alcoholic, and it's good for you."

I should've listened to my intuition and walked out of the building. Instead, I accepted a glass of passionflower juice.

The next thing I knew, I was lying on a wicker lounge in a room in the pavilion. I heard noises in the next room. The murmuring of voices, the clinking of glasses, and music. As I sat up the room blurred a little. I blinked, and the room came into focus. Four other lounges, a couple of tables cluttered with assorted party food and glasses of drink, and a large clothes rack with hangars and costumes filled the room.

As I stood, I realised I wasn't wearing my normal clothing. My jeans and shirt were on a coat hanger. How did I end up wearing a shimmering silver dress? The wooden floor felt cool beneath my bare feet. I tiptoed over to the partly closed door and peeked at the party. Around thirty people were dressed in similar fashion to the dress I wore. I recognised the four women from the committee, Brad, David, Robbie, and some older locals who must've gone to school with my parents. The other dancers didn't look familiar.

My head hurt. I rubbed my temple. Had they drugged me? Why? It made no sense. I scanned the room looking for my bag. I located it on the floor under my clothes; my shoes and socks shoved in the top of it. I checked my mobile, which told me I'd lost at least two hours sleep, maybe more. With an eye on the slightly open door, I quickly dressed. I felt less vulnerable, wearing my own clothes. I considered my next move. I wasn't ready to call the cavalry yet, until I assessed the threat level.

I peeked in at the ball. A layer of fog, not unlike the fog in the car park was beginning to form, high in the rafters of the old building. I remembered the brooch Hazel gifted me. Each morning, I tucked it in my pocket, in case of an event just like this. I pinned it on my shirt and slipped into the room where the two-piece band was playing dance tunes.

Letting my magic out, I imagined long thin tendrils searching for the source of the fog. My earth magic led me to the piano player. Mindy! Dressed in disguise as a fairytale princess, complete with a glistening golden crown, I recognised Florence's dark-haired daughter immediately. Calling my air magic, I sent the fog away, as I wiggled my fingers, causing a couple of piano wires to snap. I stood so close to Mindy I could hear her gasp as she realised what had happened. She stared right through me. I sighed with relief. The brooch worked. I hadn't thought to test it out beforehand.

Next to the piano, Cindy stopped hallway through the tune she played on her clarinet. The instrument flew from her hands and snapped into two pieces, landing with a clatter in the corner. Her medieval queen costume was even gaudier than her sisters.

Another tendril of my magic led me to the punch bowl and the table of finger food. Understanding that the food and drinks were infused with a potion, I clicked my fingers. When nothing happened immediately, I turned back to watch the partygoers. A loud crash filled the silence, as the tables laden with party food collapsed, spilling food and drink all over the polished floorboards.

Robbie stared in my direction. I almost laughed out loud at his tacky gold and red king costume. The rubies in his shiny gold crown were probably real. Beside him, Brad and David wore superhero costumes that hugged their large frames. Did anyone really think disguises like that were flattering? Their bright blue, green and black outfits certainly showed off their well-rounded figures.

I held my breath, willing him to look away. He did, beckoning Rosie and Jazz to him. Rosie and Jazz, both wore figure hugging bright red and black medieval dresses. Goddesses, queens, or witches? I couldn't figure out which they were meant to be. I moved a little closer. I couldn't hear the whole conversation, but the words *stop the meeting,* and *find something to use against her,* were clear. Instinctively I knew they meant me. I refused to let Roberto, or anyone ruin Misty Vale.

As I scanned the room my heart broke a little as I saw Shaz and Maz. Dressed in shimmering glittery gold and green dresses similar to the one I woke up in. I'd thought them friends. Thankful for my invisibility, I didn't want anyone to see the tears running down my cheeks.

Barbie and Nicholas were dressed as bikers, in black leather outfits that showed off their figures. The absence of cameras and microphones was interesting. Did the businessman not want to publicise the deals being struck during the gala event?

My instincts told me there was more than one ulterior motive for the change of date. I didn't want to risk harming anyone who attended the ball, but I wanted to make sure they weren't under a spell. I held my hands in front of me, calling on the earth, air, water, and fire as a ball of energy formed in the space between my hands. With every breath I called on spirit, to infuse healing into the ball. Gently, I tossed the shimmering orb into the air, high above the party goers. I backed out of the room as thousands of tiny sparkling stars fell from the ceiling.

As I watched from behind some trees, the pavilion disappeared. A large gazebo appeared in its place. The last of the fog from the dance room dissipated as the thousands of stars worked their magic. The attendees who five minutes earlier had been enjoying the ball, looked around as if waking up from a dream. I saw the puzzled looks on their faces. Before anyone could stop them, Robbie, Brad and David hopped into a black car parked near where the pavilion stood a few moments before. I'd restore the building, later, once I could be sure no traces of magic remained behind.

My spell had reinstated people's normal clothes. As I suspected, the fancy dress had been part of the spell to confuse and coerce the party goers. Jazz and Rosie hurried away through the tress behind the gazebo. The knots in my stomach ached, as if I'd been punched. I turned away, wanting to distance myself from the scene. As a walked away I heard Maz and Shaz, apologising to the guests. I didn't wait to hear how they proposed to make it up to them.

I thought of the four women who I considered may become friends. I had no choice but to believe they were working with Brad, David and Robbie. Not one of them had rung or sent a text asking where I was or if I was okay.

"I think they were brainwashing, or enchanting the people at the ball, to make sure more residents would side with them." I told Hazel, Ned, and Sophie an hour later. I automatically headed home after leaving the pavilion. Only after ensuring my pets were safe did I message Hazel and Ned. The four of us sat around my kitchen table. Sprinkles sat on the floor at Ned's feet, Cinnamon at my feet, with Bert happily chattering away in his cage.

"This is getting serious," Sophie said, as she wrapped her hands around the mug of hot chocolate I'd put in front of her. "Did you manage to get any actual evidence?"

I shook my head. "No, only magic, my intuition, my gut feeling, and what I overheard. I didn't think to video any of the ball, once I woke up."

"You said it was passionflower juice, that knocked you out?" Hazel asked with a puzzled look on her face.

"That's what they told me it was," I answered, thinking back to the tray with the flutes of golden liquid.

"Your father was allergic to elderberry wine, and so am I," my grandmother held her mug, and gazed at its contents. "I'm not sure how anyone would know this, but if we drank it, it knocked us out for hours."

"Did you dream or hallucinate?" Ned queried. "I only ask because maybe they were aiming to discredit Jane's account of events."

Hazel frowned, "No hallucinations, or dreams, but I slept for hours. It'd be on record at Dr Hyder's surgery."

"Doesn't Rosie work at the medical practice?" Sophie asked, scrolling through her tablet. "Yes, here it is. She works there three days a week. Rosie and Jazz have both reported several magic outbursts as cause for concern. Maz and Shaz have only reported one each."

I drew in a deep breath, exhaling slowly. "This isn't personal," I said, as images slowly moved in front of my eyes, like watching a movie reel. "It's about money, and greed. Manipulating magic to make lots and lots of money. Roberto and the Hartlys don't care about the residents, or our village, they see dollar signs. We're just collateral damage."

Chapter Twenty-Three

Not unexpectedly, Sophie and Ned received calls for assistance before we'd finished our hot chocolate. "Now that we can confirm who's behind this, we'll focus on proving, they're behaving illegally, or unethically, or both." Sophie stood, tucking her tablet into the pocket of her vest. She turned to Hazel, "Can individuals be arrested for using magic to harm or bully others?"

Hazel nodded, "If we can prove it. Which is the problem. The only way to prove magic is by using magic. Although...maybe Mikal can build a component into his programme that can trace magic residue back to the perpetrator. Leave it with me." Hazel tapped out a message on her mobile.

Ned patted my shoulder as he joined Sophie. "Are you sure you're okay?"

I smiled at Ned as I also stood. "Yes, thank you, I'm perfectly fine. It was a shock initially, that my new friends aren't who they pretend to be. I'm even more determined to rid the village of those seeking to harm us."

"And they know that you know," Hazel said with a glint in her eye. "You're not to be trifled with, granddaughter. They know this now."

My grandmother and I waved as Ned and Sophie hopped into their respective cars. "If you don't mind, I've got a meeting with Leopold, and I want to check in on Mikal's progress too."

My head was clear, my energy was buzzing, I was ready to remove the threat to our village. "I'll be busy canvasing potential council members. We can compare notes later," I added as Hazel hugged me.

With the door locked and my pets settled in the kitchen watching over me I made myself a cuppa, opened my laptop and set to work. I read through the notes I'd prepared for the meeting. I scribbled some changes. My toes wriggled in my shoes as I paced the short hallway in my cottage. Sprinkles followed me as I rolled his ball for him to play. As I topped up Bert's water Cinnamon rubbed against my legs. Once she had my attention she moved to my seat and sat beneath it.

"You're right, I'm procrastinating. Maz and Shaz's betrayal hit harder than I thought. What if the people I contact have been bullied or conned by Brad? How will I know for sure? Can I cast a spell to know for sure who isn't corrupted? Who would be the best candidates for council.

A flash of light blinked above my notepad. I returned to my seat. Six names were written in gold ink. I didn't own a pen that colour. "Thank you," I whispered to whatever magical being had answered my question.

I started with Gus Featherlight. He owned the local pet shop. His mother was an Elliott, one of the crew who were at school with my parents. He was an air elemental. Gus answered straight away. "Hello, my name's Jane Fairweather. You may have heard of me as Clara Thorne, my birth name. I'm Hazel's granddaughter. We hoped to get a chance to speak to you at the meeting last evening. Unforeseen circumstances prevented that. Would you be open to considering a role in our current council?" I sensed a hesitation on the other end of the call. "Before you answer, I assume you're aware of the current situation with regards business applications. The council isn't opposed to businesses growing and expanding, it's the intent behind the current applications concerns us."

Gus's voice cut me off, which wasn't a bad thing, as I was running out of things to say. "I'm flattered you and Hazel thought I might be a suitable candidate. Normally I'd say I'll consider it, but Brad Hartly came calling yesterday, a few minutes before I planned to head to the meeting. He provided some compelling reasons for not nominating. Thank you." I heard the click as Gus ended the call.

"So much for the golden pen of truth," I sighed. Still, my determination wouldn't let me give up just yet.

One down, five to go. Next to Gus's name in my notebook, I scribbled a few words to jog my memory when I spoke to Hazel. The next name on the list was Bernadette Wilson, water elemental and teacher at the local kindergarten. I delivered the first part of my spiel, minus the part about business applications. Bernadette sounded breathless, as if she'd rushed in from playing a strenuous game with the children. "Oh gosh, I'm flattered that you and Hazel would consider me, but no thank you." She paused, I heard her exhale, and the sound of children talking in the background. "Life's hectic as it is, but I wish you good luck with your plans." I heard the click as she hung up before I could offer any additional motivation.

I wriggled in my seat. This wasn't going well. Four names remained on the list. At least the fire elemental's last name wasn't Murphy. I dialled the number for Henry Blake. "I'd love to nominate for council." He jumped in, as soon as I finished speaking. "I was on my way to the meeting last night when a tree fell on the road in front of me. By the time I moved it and got into town I heard the meeting had been cancelled. I thought those horrible Hartlys must have gotten to you and your grandmother. The sooner we run them and their dreadful business partner out of town, the better. When do you want me to come in?"

I scanned the email I'd sent earlier that day. "We've rescheduled the meeting for 9am tomorrow morning. Did you not receive the email invitation I sent earlier?"

"No emails today, but I think there's something dodgy about the internet connection," Henry replied. "I know some people who'd be interested in attending and ridding Misty Vale of the current pests," he added. "Can I bring them along?"

"Yes, please bring along as many as you like, let people know the meeting is going ahead tomorrow. The large room in the old switchboard building." I'd not met the man, but I liked his enthusiasm and energy levels. "The best entrance is the one off the car park."

David Dean and Shelly Murphy hung up their phones as soon as I said my name. One name left. Kath Devlin. Confusingly Hazel's notes told me Kath was an earth element, having married into the Devlin family. A different branch of the family than my mother belonged to. "I'd love to come along and see what it's all about." Kat sounded curiously eager, I sensed caution as well.

Elated and exhausted I placed my mobile on the table and rose from my chair. I walked around the kitchen, getting the blood circulating after so long sitting down. Sprinkles watched, hopeful for a walk. "Not tonight, but let's get up early in the morning and walk before the meeting," I told him, rubbing the top of his head.

Two out of six wasn't so bad, considering who we were up against. I opened my fridge and stared at the empty shelves. "I really need to do a grocery shop, for here and the office. Not that I mind eating Jess's awesome café food," I told my menagerie. "After the meeting tomorrow, I'll find some time to sort that."

I sat back at the table; my eyes caught a glimpse of light emanating from my crystal ball.

Magic alone won't solve this, whispered my mother's voice. *Magic is the distraction; you are more than that.*

She's right, my father agreed. *Use logical proof, use your contacts, and your intuition.*

"They're right!" I yelled, fisting pumping the air and startling my furry and feathered brood. "Sorry guys, but why didn't I think of this before? I'm not Jane or Clara; I'm Jane and Clara!" It made sense now.

For the people in Misty Vale to believe me, that Brad and company were frauds, criminals and bullies, I needed to prove it to them. Not with words alone, or magic shows. Residents were relying on Brad and co to provide business support and money. What if I could prove they'd acquired their billions fraudulently? If I could prove bankruptcy and gaol time?

My UK friend and previous client Brett owed me a favour, although he'd paid me handsomely for my private investigative services. I sent an email to the tech giant, asking for all the information he had on Brad Hartly, David Hartly, Roberto Patri, and Robbie Banks. *Specifically financial and criminal activity, world-wide.*

Brett's reply email arrived less than thirty minutes later. *You've hit the jackpot Jane, the three men are wanted by Interpol, for the theft of several billion dollars of ancient artifacts, and several hundred million dollars they've skimmed from various shareholdings worldwide. If you can tell me where to find them, the Federal Police will arrest them for extradition to the United Kingdom to face court.*

I told Brett the men could be found in the village of Misty Vale. Within an hour he confirmed the Federal Police would arrive early the next morning. My next task was to contact Ned and my grandmother.

I've figured out a solution to our problem. I'll explain tomorrow morning. I need to create some chaos, as a distraction. You'll see some Christmas characters, and Halloween creatures come to life, temporarily. There's no danger, I want to confuse and distract Brad, David and Robbie.

Both Hazel and Ned responded positively.

It was early evening, and the sun wouldn't be going down for another couple of hours. "Come on, let's go for a walk," I told my eager pup. Cinnamon rubbed against my leg, an action I took as affirming my plans. "I'll be back soon," I told her and Bert. I felt in my pocket, my fingers confirming the brooch was there, should I require it's magic.

Sprinkles kept up as I walked briskly towards the park. Intuition told me that the best place to summon elemental magic was the open space in the middle of the village.

I call upon the water, the air, the earth, fire, and spirit to help me keep Misty Vale safe. I invoke the powers of my ancestors and the guardians of the village. Help me create chaos to save our town. Harm to no one, so mote it be.

What now? Did I expect to see giant gingerbread men and snow men to run past me? That's what happened at the end of last year. Giant Christmas creatures created havoc as they wandered around our town. I was the one who'd rid the town of the giant distractions.

My dog pulled at his lead. I let him set the direction as we walked through the park. Before long I heard the familiar giggling of two gingerbread men. The size of ten-year-old children, with red and white candy buttons, candy canes in their hands, and black lollies for eyes. A couple of snowmen chased after the gingerbread men. White as snow, black coal eyes, a carrot nose, with black top hats.

I let a smile play on my lips. "It's working," I whispered as I led Sprinkles back along the main street to our cottage. In the middle of the roundabout a group of giant grinning pumpkins rocked back and forth. Traffic slowed to a crawl as the drivers and passengers hung out the window to watch them.

Chapter Twenty-Four

"In breaking news, the quaint village of Misty Vale has once again found itself captivated by a troupe of animated storybook characters. This time it's not just snowmen and gingerbread men parading around, we've witnessed pumpkins, ghosts and witches dancing around the main streets." Barbara held the microphone out in front of Brad. "What do you propose to do about this latest example of magic gone haywire?"

The older Hartly brother took half a step back, looking over the reporter's shoulder to where three women stood dressed in long black robes, and pointy black witches' hats. "This is why we need to build the magic academy. A place where locals will learn how to properly use their magic."

Hazel, Ned and I sat outside The Milky Bar, sipping our iced coffees, watching the interview. "Sophie will bring the officers over shortly. They arrived early this morning," Ned filled us in. "I don't know how you got it all moving so quickly, but I'm looking forward to hearing the story, over a nice long uninterrupted lunch, after it's all over," he chuckled.

Minutes later, as Brad continued to speak to the camera, Sophie and the two federal police officers approached Brad, David and Robbie. Barbara motioned Nicholas to point his camera and microphone at them. She inched closer to Brad, holding her microphone out.

"Brad Hartly, David Hartly, Robbie Banks, you are all under arrest for various criminal offences, including theft and fraud. You will be extradited to the United Kingdom to face court for the offences listed within this subpoena."

"This is outrageous!" Brad interrupted, trying to snatch the paper from the federal officer.

"Preposterous!" agreed Robbie.

Barbara dressed head to toe in her signature pink tight fitting dress and ridiculously high heels, sidled up to the taller of the two uniformed men. "Excuse me officer, can you explain what's going on? These businessmen are here to help the residents of Misty Vale."

The officer slid a set of handcuffs over Brad's hands. Sophie and the other officer cuffed Robbie and David respectively. "I sincerely hope none of your residents have given these three men any money," he told Barbara gruffly. "Please turn off your recording equipment. Now," he added sternly.

"It looks like Barbie has met her match," I smiled at my companions.

"I'd better help them get those three into the van." Ned rose from his seat. "You've got a meeting to host. I can't wait to hear about it, after this circus is finally done."

The town clock chimed eight times as Hazel and I walked into our office. In all the excitement I'd forgotten to prepare the room for the meeting. "I think it's appropriate that we use our powers, to make the room as welcoming as possible for any locals who come along this morning," Hazel said as we opened the door to the meeting room. She waved her hand and the chairs I'd stacked against the wall sorted themselves into rows. Along one side of the room, a table appeared, laden with fairy cakes and bottles of water. A bowl of apples sat next to another filled with strawberries.

"Did you have something to do with what happened out there this morning?" Sharon asked as she entered the room. Joan and Steve followed behind her.

Before Hazel or I could respond, a few more people wandered in, with Barbara and Nicholas right behind them. "I think we'd all like to know the answer to that," Barbara agreed.

I glanced at Hazel. "Why don't we all sit down, Jane will fill you in on what you witnessed outside," my grandmother suggested as more people entered the space.

"I thought it was Clara, not Jane," Barbie said brightly, her fake smile plastered on for the audience.

Squaring my shoulders, I faced the group. "I was trying out my birth name. The events of the week made me realise that it doesn't matter if you know me by Jane, or Clara, I'm the same person. I have magic, and I'm an investigator. Misty Vale is my home. I'll stick with Jane, though if you want to call me Clara, I'll answer." I caught the eye of each of the locals who'd come along to meet with us. "It was my investigative skills, together with our local police officers that uncovered the truths those three men tried so hard to bury. They've each spent time in gaol, and been convicted of corporate theft, fraud, and theft of priceless ancient artefacts. Robbie Bank's real name is Roberto Patri. There are outstanding warrants for their arrest in the United Kingdom and parts of Europe."

"What about those of us who were promised help growing our businesses?" John called from the back of the room.

Hazel touched me lightly on the shoulder. "I'll answer that. The council has grant money available. If you've an idea for a business, if you've been speaking with Brad and the others, you are welcome to apply for money to help kick start your business. We have other monies available to help with farm improvements." While Hazel spoke, my mobile beeped. I checked it, hoping it wasn't Ned saying Roberto had escaped.

A smile spread across my face as I read the text from Brett. I held up my phone. "I've received notification that there was substantial reward money offered for any information that led to the arrest of those three men, Robbie in particular. I'd like to propose that any money I receive goes towards a Misty Vale business fund. We can use it to help kick start specific business plans. Of course, the details of this would have to be discussed and ratified at the council level." My eyes looked across the crowd. "Are there any other questions before we receive nominations for council?"

"Three hours! I didn't expect the town meeting would take that long," Ned commented. We were sitting in the park with Hazel, the wooden picnic table draped with a red checked cloth, on which sat three chicken wraps, a bowl of salad, three chocolate milkshakes and assorted mini cakes.

Hazel gave me a look. "You can blame my granddaughter. Once she mentioned we were receiving a huge reward for the capture of Roberto Patri, everyone wanted to nominate for council and tell us about their business idea."

I nodded, eyeing the food in front of us. "Starting on Monday we'll be interviewing candidates for council, and others for eligibility to receive grant money." The success of the meeting had surpassed my wildest expectations. Brett's message had a large part to play in that. When I'd spoken to him, he'd assured me most of the money was coming from the authorities, but that he'd added a couple of million as a token of his thanks. Apparently, he'd run into David Hartly at a charity event and had taken an instant dislike to how he conducted his business.

Ned pointed to the goodies on the table. "I suggest we eat our lunch, then go and thank Jess and her helpers for putting this together for us."

"Agreed," Hazel said, picking up the burger in front of her.

Jess's cooking was magic. There was no other word to describe the flavour burst of special sauce, slaw and seasoning.

We watched as Sophie walked across the park from the station, headed towards us. As she got closer, I saw the smile on her face. "Come and join us, there's enough dessert for everyone," I indicated spare spot next to Hazel.

"Thanks," Sophie slid in beside Grandma. "I thought you'd want to know, the three culprits are well on their way to face court overseas. Before they left, David was quick to dob in their nieces, Cindy and Mindy." She grinned as she continued, "The sisters were quick to confess they had help. The four women we know as Maz, Shaz, Rosie and Jazz were in fact all members of the Hartly and Banks corporation. Maz told us the spell at the edge of town was meant to confuse you even more, in case you suspected them." She turned to me, "I'm sorry Jane, I know you thought they were your friends."

"Only until they drugged me and tried to ruin our town," I replied.

"Quite a successful and productive day," Hazel commented, choosing a strawberry cupcake. "No wonder I'm exhausted. After this cake I'm going home to Esmerelda, and I'm not leaving home again until Monday morning." She glanced at Ned before giving me her knowing stare. "What are you up to for the rest of the weekend?"

A giggling noise stopped my reply, as three snowmen and a gingerbread man ran past, two giant pumpkins rolling along behind them. "After I remove the distractions, though they are kind of cute," I said as a couple of ghosts floated past, "I'm hoping Sophie can spare Ned for a few hours tomorrow. I have a proposal of my own." I ignored the heat rising in my cheeks as I grabbed Ned's hand. I mightn't know what the future holds, but life in Misty Vale is never dull.

The End

Sarah Lewin

If you want to know more about me or my books, here are some details. Alternatively, please make contact via any of the social media listed below:

Email: sarahlewinauthor@gmail.com

You Tube: https://youtube.com/@sarahlewinangelwisdom539

Blog: https://sarahlewin.com

Facebook: https://www.facebook.com/SarahLewinAuthorWitchyMysteryBooks

Instagram: https://www.instagram.com/sarahlewin_author/

Amazon: https://amazon.com/author/sarahlewin

Goodreads: https://www.goodreads.com/author/show/43342156.Sarah_Lewin

Book Bub: https://www.bookbub.com/authors/sarah-lewin

My Witchy Mystery Books:

<u>Witch Wisdom Series:</u>

#1 – *Crone Wisdom*

#2 – *Ancient Wisdom*

#3 – *The Wisdom of the Witches*

#4 – *Stella's Wisdom*

There are two free novellas in this series

The Coven

Kai's Story

<u>Spirit Town Cozy Mysteries:</u>

#1 – *Autumn Leaves Are Falling*

#2 – *Secrets Ghosts and Whispers*

#3 – *The Ghosts of Spirit Town*

Novella

Beth's Return

<u>Misty Vale Cozy Mysteries:</u>

#1 – *A Very Crafty Christmas*

#2 – *Magic and Mayhem in Misty Vale*

Novella

Coffee Mystery and Magic

<u>Stand Alone Books</u>

Broken Lies

<u>Anthologies</u>

Tales of the Lost Things

Tales of Whisk-ful Thinking

<u>I also have a range of children's books available, and new books set for release in 2026.</u>

My Grandma

It's Not Fair

Hidden Clues at Peppermint Farm